T0345211

RACHEL'S BLUE

THE AFRICA LIST

ZAKES MDA

Rachel's Blue

LONDON   NEW YORK   CALCUTTA

SERIES EDITOR: Rosalind C. Morris

Seagull Books, 2016

ISBN   978 0 85742 332 0

This edition is not for sale in Southern Africa

British Library Cataloguing-in-Publication Data
A catalogue record for this book is available from the British Library.

Typeset by Seagull Books, Calcutta, India
Printed and bound by Maple Press, York, Pennsylvania, USA

RACHEL'S BLUE

1

Old hippies never die, an old song suggests, they just fade away. Actually, they just drift to Yellow Springs where they've become a haunting presence on the sidewalks and storefront benches. Some in discolored tie-dyes, strumming battered guitars, wailing a Bob-Dylan-of-old for some change in the guitar case. Others just chewing the fat. Or giving curious passers-by toothless grins, while exhibiting works of art they have created from pine cones and found objects.

Jason de Klerk is too young to be one of the baby-boomer originals, though he puts a lot of effort into looking like them. He was drawn to Yellow Springs after dropping out of high school, and in that town he fell under the spell of a faded hippy called Big Flake Thomas with whom he busked at the public square or gigged at the Chindo Grille when no act with at least some regional profile had been booked. The master's fat fingers strummed and plucked on an Appalachian dulcimer, while the acolyte furiously beat a conga drum, and then blew his didgeridoo. He carried the latter instrument with him everywhere he went, slung on his shoulder, almost touching the ground and peeking just above the top of his head. In the evenings in the tiny bar of Ye Olde Trail Tavern—reputed to be Ohio's second-oldest restaurant, in operation since 1847—Big Flake took the acolyte on some nostalgic trip to an age of free love and flower power. After a few beers they staggered home under a cloud of Mary Jane. The master got high; the acolyte got stoned. And it happened like that every day. Until one day Big Flake Thomas was taken ill with pneumonia and passed on without any fuss or argument.

For Jason, Yellow Springs died with the big man. He loaded pieces of his life in his old Pontiac—and these included his mentor's fretted dulcimer, the tumbadora and the didgeridoo—and drove back home to Athens, another county famous for its aging hippy community. But, unlike in Yellow Springs, the hippies here have melted into the hills, emerging only on Wednesdays and Saturdays to sell their organic produce at the farmers' market.

It is at the farmers' market that we meet Jason loitering among the marquees, his didgeridoo on his back.

People occasionally stop to admire the black, white, and yellow lizards painted on it by an unknown Australian Aboriginal artist. Unless, of course, it is one of those ersatz products of some factory in China. He never really reflected on its pedigree since he received it as a gift from one of Big Flake Thomas's buddies who'd lost interest in the instrument with creeping age.

Jason walks past a busker—a clean-cut man on a stool, playing a guitar and singing some country song whose lyrics are on a music stand in front of him. It must be the man's own composition because Jason has never heard it anywhere before. He is selling CDs of his music. Jason would like to do that too. As soon as he gets settled he will cut a CD of some of the songs he used to play with Big Flake Thomas. It will be a wonderful tribute to his mentor, and it will also earn him a few bucks. But he will need a guitarist for that. Or at least a dulcimer player. A tumbadora and a didgeridoo on their own will not sustain the kind of performance he has in mind, let alone the recording. He has the big man's dulcimer as a keepsake, but he never learned to play it. To make it in the busking world he needs some strings. But there is no sweat about that. Someone is bound to know some adventurous guitarist, or even a banjo or mandolin player who would be willing to dabble in some experimental sounds with him.

After a few stalls of beets, kale, and zucchinis, and of candles made from beeswax and shaped into angels by a beekeeper who is also selling bottled honey, Jason stops to listen to yet another busker. She is strumming her guitar and singing "Oh, My Darling Clementine." Though her floppy straw hat covers part of her face he can see at once that she is one of those rural Ohio girls who look like milk. He concludes that it is not for her voice—rather airy and desperate—that her open guitar case is bristling with greenbacks. It is for her strawberry-blonde bangs peeping under the hat, and her deep blue eyes, and her willowy stature, and her brown prairie skirt of plaid gingham, and her bare feet with tan lines drawn by sandals, and her black tee with "Appalachia Active" in big white letters across her breasts—the entire wholesome package that stands before him in supplication. She is trying hard to make her voice sound full-bodied and round, but pity she was not born for singing. She loses a beat to say thank you after Jason deposits a single, and then she tries hard to catch up with the song before it goes out of control.

At that moment Jason recognizes her. Rachel. Rachel Boucher from Jensen Township, about ten miles or so from his Rome Township. She has grown taller and has matured quite a bit since they attended Athens High School together. She was his crush once. And for a while it looked like it would be actualized. There was a period when they spent lots of time together. To him each moment was a date—at least that's how he bragged to his buddies. To her it was just hanging out, and that's what she told the yentas—as the Yiddish-speaking math teacher from Germany called the notorious gossip-mongers—with whom she shared the lunch table. He was a class clown and therefore was popular with other boys. He would have been popular with girls too, what with his soft eyes and a friendly face—even when he thought he was scowling it looked like a smile. Girls, however, kept their distance because of his rich odor—a result of his estrangement from either shower or bath.

Rachel was the brave one who risked snide remarks for his company and jokes. "One day we gonna see you on *Saturday Night Live*," she used to tell him. Until the ribbing got into her—especially from Schuyler, the yenta queen who had taken a shine on her—and she began to have excuses when he asked her out to Movies 10 or some such place. And then one day he saw her and the yentas at the cafeteria. His tray was loaded with pizza, Tater Tots, Bosco Sticks, and milk. He smiled when he saw Rachel, but the smile froze on his lips when he heard a stage whisper: "Here comes Jason. I hope he doesn't sit at this table, otherwise I'll gag." It was Rachel. This stunned him. Of all people, not Rachel! But he soon recovered and walked with an exaggerated swag to join a bunch of loudmouthed jocks at the opposite table. Jocks are inured to body odor; they live with it every day.

Jason was facing Rachel directly, and he shoved his middle and index fingers into his mouth and pretended to gag. The mindless jocks laughed boisterously and did likewise with their fingers, even though they didn't know the reason for the apery. They thought Jason was just teasing the girls and imagined it was a good idea to join in the fun.

That's when she became aware that he had heard her. If only she could shrink herself to invisibility. She was ashamed of herself for trying to impress the yentas at Jason's expense. She did not know what possessed her to utter such words about a friend who, truth be told, she would find attractive if it were not for the little matter of hygiene. Her cruelty had been a result of trying to assure Schuyler that there was nothing between him and her, hoping that the yentas would stop referring to her behind her back as "that girl who dates the stinky kid."

Unfortunately there was no chance of her disappearing or, at the very least, of taking her words back. They had registered with Jason, and on subsequent days his bearing made it clear that he did not want to have anything to do with her. At one point she thought she should explain to Jason, and even apologize. But he was not interested in any explanation. He did not need her as a friend. For the remainder of that junior year not a word passed between them. Jason dropped out even before the senior year was over while she stayed to complete high school.

Strange that he never thought of her again. But now it all floods back as he listens to her croon "Oh, the Cuckoo!" in the manner of her mountain people. It is obvious that she does not recognize him behind all the beard, even though her eyes are fixed on his. Jason is not surprised by the fact. It's been more than five years and he has since lost his boyish look. What can be seen of his face has now been sculpted into rugged lines by the severe summers and winters of Yellow Springs. His flaxen mane is an unintended disguise; it is braided into three ropes that hang down past his shoulder under a fawn embroidered kufi hat—another inheritance from Big Flake Thomas. Red and green glass ornaments pretend to be rubies and emeralds all around the hat.

Even before the song ends Jason saunters away among the stalls.

"Play us something on your didj," a boy makes his request.

"It don't play good with a beard," says Jason without stopping.

"Then what good is it carrying it around?" asks the boy's pal.

The two boys are close on his heels.

"Yeah, and what good is your beard if you can't play the didj with it?" asks the boy, rolling his eyes.

Jason stops to glare at them.

"It's none of nobody's business," he says, and then walks away.

The boys just stand there looking at the man and his didgeridoo disappear among the cars at the parking lot.

A good woman does not resist temptation; she succumbs. That's Nana Moira's philosophy. She is really talking of candy, not of anything that would warrant the blushes of the women around the table. It is the way she says it that is suggestive. And the fact that she is a grand mature lady of eighty who is not expected to dish out double entendres so freely and unflinchingly is the source of suppressed giggles. It is because most of these young women are new to the Jensen Township Quilting Circle—their first day, in fact—and are therefore not yet used to her robust humor which is always accompanied by cackling laughter that comes even before the punch line.

Nana Moira never fails to crack herself up.

Rachel can hear her raspy voice even as she gets out of her green Ford Escort and walks into the Jensen Community Center. Nana Moira is telling the women how she has always liked Star Mints and Hershey's Kisses and she is not about to stop satisfying her sweet tooth now just because some quack tells her to take it easy on the sugar on account of her weight. But she suddenly stops when she sees Rachel walking into the room. Her hand, which was reaching for another piece of candy from a glass jar on the table, withdraws ashamedly.

"You're not even that big, Nana Moira," says one of the women.

"She's big enough to have diabetes," says Rachel sternly. "She knows she has to deal with her weight if she wants to have diabetes under control."

She is not "that big" only if you compare her weight with that of some of her neighbors who are morbidly obese. In these parts obesity is a malady of poverty. The last time Nana Moira was taken to the ER at O'Bleness the doctor said she was no longer overweight; she was obese. Now she walks with the aid of a stick, which is something new. It worries Rachel no end.

"Sweet grief, child, you not my Officer Rick," says Nana Moira. "You not my nanny either."

Officer Rick is a popular Athens policeman famous for his programs to guide teenagers to steer clear of drugs.

"I'm nobody's cop but you know you got high blood pressure and arthritis too. You got everything that kills and you don't give a damn."

Nana Moira chuckles dismissively.

"Well, I'm bound to go one day. Rather go happy than sad and blue."

Rachel hates Nana Moira when she jokes about going. She resents her already for getting sick. She wants her Nana back, the one who was hale and lusty, foraging for morels with her deep in the Wayne Forest. And this joke about going, it's no joke at all to Rachel. It's a threat. It's blackmail. This adds to the resentment that is building up in her. The resentment is so apparent that an old lady from the neighborhood once asked Nana Moira, "That ungrateful Rachel! I wonder why she's not so nice to her grandma who brought her up all by herself with nobody's help but good ol' Uncle Sam's food stamps?" But Nana Moira was not about to gossip about her granddaughter with any blabbermouth.

Rachel grabs the candy jar and pours all its contents into her handbag.

"Some kids will appreciate this," she says. "You guys, don't you bring this poison to the Center again."

The five women sitting at the table—some cutting fabric with scissors and rotary cutters, and others fiddling with uncooperative bobbins—may be new to the Circle, but they know they don't like Rachel already. She is so full of herself, they whisper among themselves when she and Nana Moira have gone to the kitchen. One makes the observation that arthritis never killed anybody, and she knows this from personal experience because her own grandma lived to be ninety-five though she practically spent a number of her later years on a wheelchair because of arthritis. What finally took her to God's own house which has many mansions was old age and not arthritis.

It would seem today is Nana Moira's day to impart skills. First there were the young women who have recently joined the Quilting Circle and were learning how to cut and sew the Irish chain, the Ohio star and the bow tie from her all morning, and now it is Rachel's turn for edification. Her grandma promised to teach her how to make the pawpaw bread that she learned from her own grandma. It never fails to get gushing compliments from the visitors at the Center every time she bakes it and puts it on the table for everyone to have a slice or two. Even those folks who profess not to care for the fruit love her bread. She was persuaded to display and sell it at the Ohio Pawpaw Festival which is an annual event in mid-September by the shores of Lake Snowden. And there, among such pawpaw delicacies as sorbet, jams, pies, beer, and sauces her bread won the hearts of the lovers of this native fruit. Rachel hopes that if she can make pawpaw bread that is half as good as Nana Moira's she will be able to sell it at the farmers' market and supplement the money she makes from her busking. People will come for the bread, listen to her music and drop a few bills into her guitar case. Or they may stop to listen to her songs and notice the bread and buy a loaf or two.

"You just do it like any other bread," says Nana Moira as she sifts the all-purpose flour and mixes it with salt and baking soda. "No big sweat."

She asks Rachel to put butter in the mixer and cream it. Under her direction Rachel adds sugar, then eggs, and continues beating the mixture until it is fluffy. She adds the flour, mashed pawpaw pulp and hickory nuts. She then places the dough in the oven. As it slowly bakes, Rachel and Nana Moira go back to the sewing room to join the quilters. But the women are already calling it a day and packing the fabric and sewing machines away.

"Don't leave before you taste my bread," says Rachel. "I need your expert opinion."

"We got things to do," says one of the women abruptly.

They say goodbye to Nana Moira and leave.

"Did I say something?"

"They think you're a party pooper, that's all," says Nana Moira. "They don't know my sweet little girl, that's why."

"Am not a little girl anymore, Nana Moira."

"Sweet Jesus! It don't matter how old you think you are, Rachel. You'll always be my little girl."

"Party pooper! What party did I poop on?"

Nana Moira bursts out cackling and says, "They don't like folks who confisicate my Hershey's Kisses."

"Confiscate, Nana Moira."

"That's what I said."

Rachel does not respond. Instead she busies herself with paging through Monday's issue of the *Athens News* while Nana Moira spreads cut pieces of cloth on a long white table for the next quilt she will be stitching together.

The loaf is rosy brown when Rachel takes it out of the oven an hour later. She covers it with a cloth and asks Nana Moira to share it with her Center regulars and visitors tomorrow. She will return on Friday to bake a number of loaves for the Saturday market. And she will do that every week for the rest of the pawpaw season.

"I've a surprise for you in your room," says Nana Moira as Rachel gets into her car.

Their home is only half a mile from the Center. It is a double-wide, much bigger than the other five trailers that form a row. Unlike the rest which are in bad shape with peeling paint and gutters that need fixing, Rachel's trailer is glistening with new paint. Its surroundings are clean and neat with cottage pinks and tomatoes growing in pots. The big satellite dish on the roof makes it look like a space ship from some awkward sci-fi movie.

Rachel parks her car on the paved driveway in front of the trailer, making sure that she leaves enough space for Nana Moira to park her 1983 GMC Suburban when she returns in the evening. To Rachel's consternation she still drives at night at her age, and loves speed. These days she struggles to climb into the car since it has become too high for her arthritic knees. But she won't give it up or trade it for a lower car; it belonged to her late husband.

The mobile home is just as neat inside, and smells of Febreze in every room. Rachel goes straight to her room, the master bedroom that used to belong to her parents. When Nana Moira came to live with them after her late husband's creditors obtained a default judgment and foreclosure decree on her truck farm, she took the smaller bedroom and filled the third bedroom on the roof with boxes of all the sentimental stuff she owned. Those days Rachel used to sleep on the sofa-bunk-bed that is still in the living area in front of the television.

Since then Rachel has upgraded the place, fixed new tiles in the bathroom and shower, and bought a new propane-operated stove in the kitchen area. It is rarely in operation though because Nana Moira does most of the cooking at the Center and brings the food home in the evening.

In the bedroom Rachel is greeted by a rag doll sitting perkily on top of her pillow as if it owns the place. At first she cannot believe her eyes, and then she shrieks and reaches for it.

"Blue! My Blue! Where've you been?"

Blue is still in the blue frock as Rachel remembers her. A blue frock, a black cape and a black bonnet.

She holds her close to her bosom. She had forgotten all about Blue since she went missing a few years back. Just like she forgot all the others who had disappeared. She had mourned, and moved on. But here's Blue—she has come back. None of the others have.

She was four or five when she first got Blue. She had always wanted a Raggedy Ann and had badgered her father for it. One day he—an itinerant musician and teller of tall tales—was traveling through Amish country when he chanced upon a roadside stall with rag dolls of different sizes. He bought one for his little girl.

The first time Rachel saw the doll she freaked out.

"It's no Raggedy Ann, Pops," she had cried.

"It's a rag doll, what's the difference?" asked her father.

"It has no eyes or mouth or nose or ears or nothing. It's creepy."

"It has no face because it's an Amish doll, baby. Them Amish believe all folk are the same in the eyes of God. So they don't do faces on their dolls."

This explanation, however, did not comfort Rachel. She couldn't bring herself even to look at the doll without a face. Until her father drew eyes, a nose and a mouth with a ballpoint pen. Though they were crude like those one would see on a stick figure drawn by a child, Rachel accepted them, and gradually she learned to love the doll. It became her constant companion.

As a kid Rachel showered all her love on Blue. Sometimes all her anger. When she had tantrums she repeatedly hit the floor with Blue, and Blue took all the abuse uncomplainingly. She was made of sturdy stuff. The Amish stitches were tough and Blue did not fall apart.

After her father died in Operation Desert Storm, Rachel grew even more attached to the doll and held on to it everywhere she went. Even to kindergarten. Though they didn't allow kids to come with their own toys to school the teacher made a special exception for Rachel and her Blue because "this kid has issues." As a result she was picked on by bratty kids.

When Nana Moira and Rachel's mom met Rachel at the bus stop, she was in tears.

"They called me a rutter," she cried.

"What the fuck is a rutter?" asked her mom who was not quite sober at that time of the afternoon.

"That's what they call hillbilly kids in Athens. After some poor family called the Rutters way back in the day," explained Nana Moira whose work at the Jensen Community Center exposed her to all sorts of gossip.

"This ain't no hillbilly doll. It's an Amish doll. They're too dumb to know the difference," said Rachel's mother, glaring at her mother-in-law as if Nana Moira was the originator of the "rutter" idea.

"It's not about the doll. It's about us 'cause we poor," said Nana Moira.

That was before Rachel's mom lost her teeth to meth, and then her mind, and wandered away with a fellow meth-head, never to return. The people of the township said it was a result of a broken heart after she lost her husband who had enlisted because, as he said, "The music business ain't paying them bills and some bad folks are crapping on America in Kuwait."

When everyone was gone, Blue was the only one that stayed. There was Nana Moira of course, but she didn't count that much. She spent the whole day working at the Center's Food Pantry, or traveling to Logan to get more food from the Food Bank. Blue, on the other hand, was always with Rachel. She was not apt to die in a war or disappear in a fog of drugs.

Although Nana Moira tried to be with Rachel as much as possible, she spent her time mostly at the Center unloading food from the trucks, dividing the cans and vegetables into many equal parcels and giving them out to long lines of people who would not survive without the Food Pantry. Or cooking in the kitchen of the Center for the senior citizens of the township. Or sewing quilts with the women of the Quilting Circle. Or poring over papers and receipts and vouchers. And all that time Rachel played alone under the long tables, or on the porch, weather permitting, inventing games with Blue.

It is after nine when Nana Moira hobbles in with a small pot of bean soup.

"I know you gonna bitch about my driving at night," she says. "Save your breath already and eat the bean soup."

But Rachel is in no mood for a confrontation.

"Where was she at?" she asks, holding Blue up.

"In the storeroom. I found her when I was looking for something else."

"You knew all the time where she was at?"

"I forgot where she was at."

Nana Moira reminds her that there was a time when Rachel was collecting and piling up stuff. She didn't want to part with anything, however useless it was, so Nana Moira began to take things away from her as soon as they seemed to accumulate. Empty ice-cream containers, plastic spoons, and Styrofoam boxes—all found their way into the garbage can despite Rachel's tantrums. That gave Nana Moira the idea about the doll—if she could take away the stuff, she could take away the doll too.

"You was at middle school already, still attached to that raggedy thing. Everyone said it was unnatural, so I hid it away." Soon Nana Moira forgot in which of the many boxes she had placed the doll.

Rachel has a vague memory of her hoarding days which are a far cry from who she is today, a woman obsessed with neatness and clean surroundings. She remembers how devastated she was when Blue went missing. Blue was with her when she was a latchkey kid. She had granted her comfort and security in times of loneliness and longing. And then all of a sudden Blue was gone. Like all those who left. Fortunately middle school had become hectic with new friends who did not call her a rutter, among them Schuyler who is her best friend to this day. And lots of social activities. Choral society, drama club, boys, birthday parties, sleep-overs—you name it. Blue became a fading memory.

And now she has returned. The ballpoint-pen drawings of the eyes, nose, and mouth have long faded and Blue is faceless again. But Rachel is not scared of her anymore; Blue is no longer creepy. She tells Nana Moira so, and they both laugh at what a silly kid she was to be spooked by a faceless doll.

"I hope you won't be obsessing on that rag doll again," says Nana Moira jokingly.

"Come on, Nana Moira, I'm not a kid anymore. She's just a good keepsake now because Pops bought her for me."

Nana Moira is pleased to hear this. When she discovered Blue she debated with herself as to whether she should give the doll back to Rachel or keep it hidden forever or even get rid of it. What if she became fixated again on the darn thing? She decided to take the risk since Rachel is now a woman of twenty-three who has developed other interests. Thankfully, Rachel is confirming that her decision was the right one.

Some of those "other interests" that she has developed over the years, however, worry Nana Moira. She had hoped that Rachel would go further with her learning after completing high school at eighteen with mostly As and one or two Bs. She would have been the first in the family to go to college. But Rachel was taken up by music—something that runs in the family but that Nana Moira had hoped would bypass Rachel.

"This singing thing is not working out. You been doing it for five years and it's taking you nowhere," she nagged Rachel.

But Rachel had a highly romanticized notion of her father singing and telling tall tales at county fairs. She wanted to be like him, or, better still, be a recording star.

She had an even more romanticized view of her grandpa, Nana Moira's husband, whom people talk about with nostalgia to this day, more than a decade since he passed on. Nana Moira has inadvertently reinforced that view by narrating with great relish at the slightest provocation the good old days when Robbie was a country-and-western singer who played a guitar in his own group known as the Jensen Band. He played in dance halls and at social occasions, and Nana Moira and the other young ladies of the township went square-dancing every weekend in their colorful gingham square dance dresses and circle skirts. The fifties were crazy years for Moira and Robbie Boucher and for every young couple in Jensen Township. It didn't matter if it snowed or not, the Jensen Band traveled to dance halls all over the county, even as far as Meigs and Washington counties. On occasion they would stop in the middle of the road and square dance in the snow.

But Robbie also played his guitar—sometimes the mandolin or the fiddle—at home for Nana Moira and the kids. It didn't matter whether there was an audience or not, he sat on the porch and played and hummed and sang and yodeled and field-hollered. Neighborhood kids often came and joined in sing-alongs until their moms yelled for them because it was already dark and the stars were shining in the sky.

"Anyone playing or just loving music was right up his alley," Nana Moira said. "He took after his mom and pops because they played music too. For generations and generations the Bouchers was always music people."

At this Nana Moira got misty-eyed, and then she broke out laughing.

"We all loved Robbie's music—it is one thing I miss about him. One of my favorite songs that he played was 'Burn Down the Barn and Boil the Cabbage.' It was a very romantic song."

This brought out derisive laughter from Rachel.

"Yecchy! Boil the cabbage!" she screeched. "How did it go?"

"It didn't have words. Just guitar. But, Sweet Jesus, it was a mighty pretty tune."

The boys of the band often came to the house to play with him. Nana Moira loved to entertain and there would be lots of eating and singing and dancing. If it was too hot or too cold, the festivities would be in the barn. Maybe that's where she got the bug to entertain senior citizens and all the other folks of Jensen Township at the Center with dinners and lunches on special occasions such as Valentine's Day, Thanksgiving, and Fourth of July.

"No wonder I like music so much—I lived around it for years," said Nana Moira. "That's how your pops got infected with the music bug."

"That's how I got infected too," said Rachel.

"Sweet grief, child, you weren't there in the ol' days."

"Pops got infected from good ol' Robbie and I got infected from Pops. That's how it goes, Nana Moira."

Rachel grew up with these stories and she loved them. They confirmed to her that she was born to follow the family tradition. No one had the heart to tell her that her voice was not nearly as easy on the ear as her dad's and grandpa's. It didn't matter as long as she played the guitar and sang for the joy of it.

But when she spoke of making music her life, Nana Moira began to be concerned. The girl had so much potential to bring glory to the family in other ways, and she nagged her about going to college.

Rachel had a dream and was going to pursue it no matter what.

There was a time when Nana Moira thought she had finally prevailed on her, and Rachel agreed to consider going to college. Nana Moira hoped that perhaps after years of struggling as a wannabe music star she had come to realize that the dream was not materializing. She brought brochures from Hocking College and they pored over them. She decided on a two-year associate degree in addiction counseling, because her mom was destroyed by meth.

"Not that I'm giving up on my music altogether," she told her grandma. "Otherwise I would be giving up on my heritage. I would be betraying my genes."

She was planning to be a singing counselor, using her guitar as therapy to bring the meth-heads, pot-heads and crack-heads of southeast Ohio back to the road of clear-headedness and healing. She did not know if this was possible or even acceptable in that profession, but it was the only way to harness her heritage to this new cause.

"Whatever," said Nana Moira.

As long as the girl went to school, that was all that mattered to her. When she got to Hocking College and came face to face with the real world, she would give up all the singing-counselor silliness.

Nana Moira got worried when weeks went by and Rachel was not completing the forms and submitting the application. She kept on finding this and that excuse. Until finally she confessed that her heart was not on college—not at that moment. Perhaps some time in the future she would consider it.

Nana Moira knew that there would be no time in the future. She might as well give up on any notion of having the first college graduate in the Boucher family and be stuck with another itinerant musician—and this time a very bad one.

"Don't be so sad about it, Nana Moira," said Rachel. "Hocking College can do without my money. I'd rather use it to take care of you."

Rachel is the only one who brings in some reasonable livelihood home, thanks to her busking. Everyone at the Jensen Community Center is a volunteer, even Nana Moira. The only reward for her selfless work is the free food that she gets from the Food Pantry and a small stipend that is far below minimum wage.

"Sweet grief, child, I don't need nobody to look after me," said Nana Moira adamantly. "I managed alright from the time you was little without your help."

It is not just Rachel's music that Nana Moira worries about. After all, she is taking after the rest of the Bouchers before her and there is nothing anyone can do about that. Perhaps she should just accept it. But now Rachel—and Nana Moira blames Schuyler's bad influence for this—has taken to running around all over the county at her own expense, attending meetings and yelling slogans against the government, which is none of her business. She has joined Appalachia Active, a group of concerned citizens of southeast Ohio who protest fracking.

Nana Moira complains that Rachel spends too much time attending anti-fracking demonstrations instead of focusing on the more important things in her life. She is afraid that one day the law will come knocking at the door to tell her that her granddaughter is in jail for chaining herself to fracking equipment. That's the sort of thing these crazy people do; you read such stories in the *Athens News* all the time. Or worse, she may end up like Schuyler.

Although Rachel refuses to discuss Schuyler, Nana Moira has heard the gossip that she is either doing time or has done time for some crime and is now crippled for life because of her wayward behavior with men. Not that Rachel is one of these man-crazy girls you see running around with other people's husbands. No, not her Rachel. She is raised too well for that. But with a friend like Schuyler, who knows what bad influence she may exert on her?

Rachel is very headstrong. Stubborn just like her father. Whenever Nana Moira talks to her about this anti-fracking business and about Schuyler's bad influence, she throws a tantrum and tells her grandma to mind her own business, that she is not a kid anymore and should be left alone to make her own decisions. She says she is entitled to her own mistakes. Whoever heard such moonshine?

2

Members and supporters of Appalachia Active, and just some curious citizens, have assembled in the Arts West theater building. Rachel sits at the front pew—this used to be a church some years back before the community bought it as a multipurpose performance space; it still has rows of pews for theater seats. She is among a group of young women from the city and outlying townships. She sits next to Schuyler, her best friend from Rome Township. Occasionally they throw a glance at the two men and two women at a table on the stage, but most of their attention is on the people who are trickling in, filling the pews.

"Hey, there is Jason. You remember him, don't you? We called him the stinky kid," says Schuyler, looking at the two men walking the aisle and looking for space on opposite pews. One of them is Jason and the other is Genesis de Klerk, his father.

"I didn't. You and the other yapping yentas called him that," says Rachel. "Is that him? Where has he been?"

"Yapping yenta" elicits screams of excitement from Schuyler, and the girls forget all about Jason as they reminisce about high school and the lisping teacher who gave Schuyler and her friends that label because indeed they were busybodies. They mimic the teacher and the other young women on the pew join the conversation with their own memories of the trouble they used to get into as a result of not minding their own business.

One of the women on the stage, the older one, uses her clenched fist as a gavel to call the meeting to order and the assembly falls silent. She welcomes everyone to the workshop, especially the visitors from West Virginia who have come to help the people of Athens organize against the fracking companies.

"I always have a flashback of the sixties when I'm with members of Appalachia Active," she says, rubbing her hands together with glee.

She then introduces everyone on the stage: the young woman is from the university where she recently graduated with an engineering degree; and the man is a legal practitioner in Athens, "a lawyer to love" because he fought for the Wayne Forest. Everyone laughs at the characterization of the handsome middle-aged man because lawyers are generally reputed to be unlovable. This is quite a good generational mix because the fourth facilitator on the stage is a young man, Skye Riley, perhaps in his early twenties, who is a coal miner from West Virginia.

The young engineer is the first to address the meeting. She is using Microsoft PowerPoint to illustrate what hydraulic fracturing is all about. She tells the assembly that fracking technology has been in existence for sixty years, but horizontal drilling is a new technology.

"You get oil and gas, but you also get a lot of waste water that no one knows what to do about," she says.

She shows slides of the different classes of wells and explains in detail how water is injected into them and the potential for pollution these present. Then she talks about the abandoned and orphaned wells throughout southeast Ohio and the ground-water contamination that they cause, besides the fact that they are great conduits of this poison to the surface.

Although this is called a workshop, it is really a lecture. All the technical stuff cannot hold Rachel's attention for much longer and she begins to fidget. Her eyes wander and catch Jason de Klerk gazing at her. He smiles. She smiles back.

People have lots of questions after the engineer's presentation. Rachel is most impressed by her age; she is definitely younger than Rachel and yet here she is on stage addressing all these people, talking with eloquence and authority, and teaching people far older than her, some of whom are respected professionals in the county, things they knew nothing about. Because of her education she is more of an asset to Appalachia Active than Rachel is. All of a sudden she now sees her role as only to increase the numbers at demonstrations and protest marches. She does not add much value to the organization. Nana Moira was right, she concludes—she must go back to school. She may not be an engineer like the young lady, but she can also be someone whom people look up to. She is even more impressed when the engineer answers the questions with confidence and humor, and with how she tries to be fair and honest. When she has no information on the advantages and disadvantages of a specific fracking method, she says so, and directs the questioner to other sources that are more knowledgeable than her.

The lawyer to be loved takes the stage with more panache. Perhaps he imagines he is addressing the jury. He talks of well blow-outs that release millions of gallons of polluted water into creeks, of how natural water streams are hit when fracking companies prepare the ground for fracking, and of numerous occasions when the valves of trucks are "accidentally" left open so that the brine can be spilled along the road. All the while he gives specific examples of towns, villages, and townships where these things have happened, and what the response or lack of response of Ohio government agencies was.

This angers the people; some yell that this must not be allowed to happen. Rachel steals a glance at Jason. She catches him still staring at her. She wonders if he is paying attention to the proceedings at all. She finds his gaze discomfiting. He waves furtively. She responds with a weak smile and quickly redirects her eyes back to the stage.

"Every well in Athens County is an old well that has been converted, most before we even had laws," says the lawyer, before outlining what legal recourse the communities have. It becomes obvious to Rachel that his role is to teach Appalachia Active how to get around things, how to stay within the law in their protests, how to use the loopholes in the law to fight against fracking companies. He was arming the members with legal tools on how to beat the fracking industry at its own game. He has really studied the law as it pertains to extractive industry and has explored the many avenues that aggrieved communities can follow to take their cases to the Ohio Department of Natural Resources, to city and county officials, to state representatives, to the state governor, and to the courts.

The chairperson seems to have a different view, at least that's what her facial expression shows as the lawyer uses PowerPoint slides to sum up his legal argument. She does not directly challenge him though. After he has answered a few questions from the assembly and taken his seat, she calls upon Skye Riley to make his presentation. When he stands up, one can see how scrawny he looks, yet he moves and gesticulates as though he has just been ejected from a dynamo. His is not a meticulously prepared PowerPoint presentation. He just speaks off the cuff.

"We can't play by their rules," he says. "They are pillaging our land and poisoning our water. We need direct action."

The audience is immediately electrified, especially the front pew of young women. Rachel is all agog.

"You can actually change the situation you live in without dealing with politicians," Skye Riley continues. "You need no one's permission to confront the industry that is killing our families. We can't wait for two years dealing with the courts—we need direct action now."

There is a long applause. The lawyer is trying very hard to hide his wounded look behind a smile. But it is a very mechanical smile. He takes the young man's utterances as a personal attack on him.

"Direct action," someone shouts from the floor, "what does it mean exactly?"

All eyes turn on the heckler. It is Genesis de Klerk.

"It means you chain yourselves to pieces of equipment," says Skye.

Everyone knows exactly what he is talking about. Some people are already resorting to that cause of action. An Appalachia Active member is currently on trial for doing exactly that. The news has been on Power 105 FM and on *Athens News.* It is what scared Nana Moira—the way things are going, Rachel may suffer the same fate.

"It means you sit in the governor's office and refuse to leave. It takes endless energy and money to go into the community organizing. Slow and patient work needs resources and time, which we don't have. In West Virginia, we decided direct action is the only solution. We can't wait for state regulatory bodies to work."

The young women are screaming like Skye is some rock star. The young men are clapping and nodding their heads in agreement. Jason is unimpressed. His attention is on the women on the opposite front pew.

"He's been staring at you all this time, dude," Schuyler whispers to Rachel.

"He's not staring at anybody. He's speechifying."

"Come on, you know I'm talking of Jason."

"How do you know he's staring at me and not you?"

"You were his girlfriend, not me."

Rachel elbows Schuyler on the rib cage, and they giggle.

Skye Riley is looking directly at them; they fall silent and pay attention. He is explaining that extractive industries affect poor people everywhere. People who are doing mountaintop mining in West Virginia are the same people who are poisoning Ohio waters through fracking. They are also the people who are driving poor folks of color out of their houses in New Orleans.

"We need people who are willing to lock themselves to equipment. We need folks who are not afraid to go to jail," he says before sitting down to even greater applause.

"Shut down the injection wells in Ohio now!" some people are chanting.

It is obvious that most people in the room agree with the direct action route and some may even personally commit themselves to it. Rachel finds the chants electrifying. Such gatherings are what make life so wonderful in Athens County.

The girls agree that Skye Riley is "awesome," especially when he glowers at the mention of elected officials who have sold out to extractive industry. When he shapes his lips into a defiant smirk he is even more "cute." They both admit to each other that they fancy him, although it is all in jest and laughter. Rachel is happy that Schuyler is gradually coming out of her shell and is becoming herself again after the death of her lover and then a trial that left her broken-spirited and on probation. She is beginning to appreciate life and men again. But the fact that she has a permanent limp and will walk with the aid of a crutch for the rest of her life will be a constant reminder of that sad chapter in her life.

After the meeting Skye rushes out for a much-needed smoke as the rest of the people mill about the aisle debating the merits of direct action versus legal channels. Genesis is obviously a rule-of-law guy. He says he believes in protest, orderly demonstrations, and court actions rather than in this so-called direct action which to him is tantamount to violent revolution. An elderly woman says Genesis is living proof of how people change as they age. After all, he is no stranger to jail; back in the day he used to lead sit-ins and lie-ins and other kinds of defiance campaigns against every cause known to man—ranging from the Vietnam War to the saving of seals and whales and all sorts of animals that don't even exist in America. A fellow sixties'-hippy—an unre-constituted one—asks, "When did Genesis become so conservative?"

"Bullshit, you guys just want West Virginia folks to take over our fight," says Genesis, looking around for Jason. "Let's go, Jase."

Jason bumps into Rachel.

"Excuse me," says Rachel.

"You're excused," says Jason. "Although I should be the one to apologize."

"Jason!" she says.

"Yep, the one and only. Good to see you're as pretty as you ever was."

She doesn't say "thank you." Compliments always embarrass her.

"Meet my pa."

"You're Nana Moira's girl," says Genesis.

He shakes her hand heartily. "How's the grand ol' lady?"

"She's doin' great, Genesis. I didn't know you were Jason's dad," says Rachel. "I knew him way back in high school."

Rachel only got to know Genesis de Klerk a few years ago when Jason was already playing a hippy in Yellow Springs. He never talks about a son when he visits the Jensen Community Center just to hang out with the other seniors and gossip about the good ol' days or to donate fresh produce for Nana Moira's Food Pantry. She and Nana Moira have been to Genesis's house, deep in the Wayne Forest, to glean tomatoes from his vast garden. Nana Moira makes them into salsa. He is the most organic of all the old hippies of southeast Ohio. His home is self-sufficient in almost everything including electricity which he gets from solar panels that are on the roof and on the boulders in the wild-looking part of the garden. Behind the house is a dam where he catches his fish. There are a few bee-hives for honey, ducks and chickens for eggs and meat, a cow for milk, and three large heaps of compost.

What Rachel remembers most about the visit is when she wanted to use the bathroom, Genesis's wife—Rachel now concludes she cannot be Jason's mom, judging by her young age, but his stepmom—took her to a room with a wooden toilet seat and a portable bucket under it. The family does all its business in that room and in another one like it downstairs. The contents are emptied outside and become part of the compost heap. That's what gets Genesis's vegetables so gigantic and full of vigor.

Rachel cannot forget how she flipped out. She had not known that some people use crap to fertilize their gardens.

"Nothing more organic than human crap," Nana Moira told her when they were driving home.

"I'm not gonna eat Genesis's veggies. Otherwise I am gonna think of all that crap. I wonder why it didn't smell in the house, not even in the latrine."

"Maybe they treat it with something that eats the smell," said Nana Moira.

"You going to eat those veggies even when you know they've been fertilized with Genesis's crap?"

"Of course. I eat them all the time. We've been eating them all along and we're as healthy as a fiddle."

"Not me, Nana Moira. Not anymore."

"You don't know what manure they use for veggies from Kroger or from the Food Bank."

That flipped Rachel even more. To this day she hates vegetables.

But it is not from the vegetables, honey, eggs, and milk that Genesis's family earns its livelihood. These are mostly for home consumption. Genesis buys a lot of cheddar from Wisconsin cheese mongers and adds value to it by aging it before selling it at the farmers' market. Rachel and Nana Moira were impressed once when he took them to his cellar and showed them the shelves with chunks of cheese in half-open glass containers or just wrapped in wax paper. There were thermometers on the walls and a range of fans on the floor to create air circulation. Some of the cheese, he told them, had been there for two years and would only be sold after another three to fetch a good price from connoisseurs. Rachel was struck by the smell that permeated the room, both moldy and pungent, almost like pee in a musty room—a smell that she has associated with Genesis and his wife ever since. Even as he stands here with his son and Schuyler, she can detect the familiar whiff.

"You remember Schuyler?" says Rachel to Jason.

"Yeah. The queen of them yentas back in the day."

The memory provokes a few giggles; Genesis is bemused.

"'Back in the day' being the operative words here," says Schuyler.

"I'll leave you with your friends, Jase," says Genesis. "Some of us have to work."

Jason suggests they all go for coffee at Donkey provided they give him a ride home. He was persuaded to attend this meeting by his dad, so he came with him in his car.

Rachel helps the limping Schuyler down the steps.

And there is Skye Riley sitting on the steps smoking a cigarette.

"You girls didn't hear a darn thing I was saying. Talking all the time," he says looking at Rachel and Schuyler. And then turning to Jason he adds, "I bet you can't get a word in edgeways with these two, bro."

"About chaining ourselves," says Schuyler, "that's what we were talking about."

"In that case you're forgiven," says Skye.

He stands up to introduce himself, and they all laugh and tell him they already know who he is. After they have told him their names, he says he hopes to see them at the Appalachia Active's first ever Action Camp that will be held in a month or so at the old Stewart School. It will be a community weekend of workshops about injection wells, fracking, community organizing, and direct action, all aimed at helping activists from all over southeast Ohio to prepare themselves for the impending fight. He will come all the way from the Blue Ridge Mountains to facilitate some of the workshops. Jason and Schuyler say they will not be able to attend the camp, but Rachel will definitely be there. Skye is excited to hear this and promises that he will see her there.

Jason, Schuyler and Rachel walk to Rachel's Ford Escort which is parked on the street just in front of the building.

"Holy fuck, these guys take themselves so seriously," says Jason when the three of them are seated at Donkey sipping coffee. "You're not chaining yourselves to no frackin' shit, will ya?"

Rachel says she will because she believes in the cause. Schuyler, on the other hand, would not be able to even if she wanted. She is on probation and is still doing community service for a crime that the county prosecutor called "aggravated stupidity." For the past few years she had a passionate affair with a married man whose promises to leave his wife and be with Schuyler forever and ever were never fulfilled. Instead he died in a motorcycle accident. Schuyler was on the pillion when this happened.

Schuyler was at O'Bleness Hospital when the man was cremated. After months of hospitalization she is now in physiotherapy.

The man's family barred her from visiting his remains that were kept in an urn in a columbarium at the cemetery. This embittered her because, as she told Rachel, all she wanted was to say goodbye to her lover. So one night she took a cab to the cemetery—she didn't want to involve Rachel in the crime she was planning—and broke the glass front of the niche with a rock. She grabbed the urn and fled. Out on the road she phoned another cab to pick her up.

The wife knew immediately that this was not an act of random vandalism. She told the police who she suspected, and indeed they found the man's ashes in Schuyler's bedroom, on the nightstand next to her bed. She told the officers that she stole the man's ashes because he was hers and his wife had no business keeping them or barring her from the cemetery. She was adamant that the man loved her, not the wife, and the fact that when he died he was with Schuyler was proof enough. Therefore she felt that she was more entitled to those ashes than the official widow. This was Schuyler's defense at the Athens Court of Common Pleas where she was on trial for felony vandalism. She was convicted and sentenced to a two-thousand-five-hundred-dollar fine and community service. She is still serving that sentence and if she were to be caught on the wrong side of the law again during her period of probation, she would certainly go to prison. That's why she is not prepared to take any risk chaining herself to fracking equipment even though, like her friend Rachel, she strongly believes in the cause.

"But I heard you chant 'direct action, direct action' major," says Jason.

"Yeah, I can chant it 'cause I support it, but I can't do it," says Schuyler.

Both Rachel and Schuyler find Jason a pleasant guy, a gentleman in fact, despite his vocabulary which is peppered with cuss words and has regressed from the high-school-acquired register to that of the township folks who don't have much schooling. He tells them about his carefree life in Yellow Springs, his sadness at the loss of Big Flake Thomas, and his return to old Athens County where he hopes to resuscitate the music career that was really coming along fine in Yellow Springs until the big man decided to join celestial buskers.

In the meantime, he is helping his father in his cheese-aging business and he hates it. He has come to hate cheese in all its manifestations, and as soon as he finds a job, he's bailing out on his father.

What bugs him most is that his father has lately discovered God after a life as an agnostic hippy. He has gone back to the religion of his Michigan-Dutch ancestors—the Reformed Church in America—and has the religious fervor of a new convert that tends to annoy everyone around him. For instance, on Thanksgiving his relatives from Michigan descended like the Elders of Zion to Rome Township and turned his home into a revivalist retreat.

Rachel remembers that Genesis's origins are traced back to Michigan. His father—Jason's grandfather, that is—was a pipe fitter and welder of Michigan-Dutch stock who came from Grand Rapids to work at the booming coal mines in Rome Township in the 1940s. In the beginning he had stood out as a foreigner because people here have close-knit families with bloodlines that are identifiable from their surnames. But he worked his way into the heart of the community and soon his strange Michigan-Dutch surname was as native as the Appalachian soil.

"It can't be that bad," says Rachel. "You're just set in your wild Yellow Springs ways."

"Nothing wild about Yellow Springs. It's a place of art and culture. Carefree ways, yes, not wild ways. Major carefree! But here, I'm like a slave. I'm a grown-ass man but Pa treats me like I'm a kid still."

He goes along with the treatment just to please his pa and make his step-ma, whom he adores, happy. As soon as he returned from Yellow Springs they took him to Grand Rapids to be baptized into the church of his ancestors. He went along with that too; it made them happy and saved him from any nagging that was sure to come from his pa.

He was christened Revelation, in the name of the Father, the Son, and the Holy Ghost.

"Revelation as in the Book of Revelation?" asks Schuyler, laughing.

"From Genesis to Revelation," says Rachel.

"I hate that name. I am Jason, and I don't wanna be a cheese-monger. I wanna be a music-monger."

"Those, my friend, are lyrics of a new song," says Rachel.

"You can play together," says Schuyler. "You'll make a great team."

"Holy fuck! You got it, Schuyler. Right there, you got it major. Please say yes, Rachel. I heard you play at the farmers' market the other day. We can make something good."

Rachel thinks this is just talk. She doesn't evince any enthusiasm for the suggestion. In any event she never had any plans to team up with anyone. She is a solo artist. Like her dad. Like her granddad. Okay, her granddad was not solo all the time. He had a band. The Jensen Band. But even then, it was "Robbie and the Jensen Band."

"We can do it, Rachel. Me and my conga and my didj. You and your guitar. You don't need to sing nothing.

Just play the guitar. We'll produce sounds that no one in these parts has ever heard. Think about it, man, think about it."

"There's nothing to think about," says Schuyler. "You two were meant for each other. She's going to do it, Jason. I know she will. She's got too much sense not to do it."

After an afternoon of banter and laughter, Jason says he won't need the ride home after all. He wants to go bar-hopping on Court Street. He's going to celebrate the new partnership that he hopes will come to fruition as soon as Rachel gives a positive answer.

"Dude, you think I don't see what you're up to pushing me to this guy?" says Rachel as she drives on Route 50, taking Schuyler home.

"For music, dude. Only for music. Don't you get any dirty ideas further than that."

They agree that Jason has become a very charming and well-turned-out man, a far cry from the stinky kid they knew at high school.

Nana Moira agrees to let Jason work at the Center as a volunteer. This means he is not earning any wage but will occasionally get a few dollars as gas money. It took Rachel days of cajoling for Nana Moira to finally go along with this arrangement. She did not want to get on the wrong side of Genesis, a man who has donated a lot to the Food Pantry, helping it not to depend solely on the supplies from the Food Bank in Logan.

Jason takes to his tasks with gusto. He can be seen with a bucket and a mop, cleaning the linoleum floors without anyone asking him to do so. He even dusts the furniture, a thing that no one ever did at the Center. When Nana Moira needs some ingredients for her culinary masterpieces, he volunteers to drive to Wal-Mart in the city in his Pontiac, a distance of more than twenty miles. And he always returns promptly with the right stuff. Soon Nana Moira becomes dependent on him and misses him on the days he hasn't come.

He has no obligation to be at the Center at all, but he is there on most days of the week. Sometimes there is no work for him, so he just sits at the long tables and gossips with the quilting women. Once in a while Rachel is there and joins in the gossip. Thanks to Jason the new quilting women are beginning to open up to her, to realize that she is not such a snooty person after all. She, on the other hand, betrays a tinge of jealousy when they hover over Jason and hold on to every word he utters.

People notice that whenever Genesis stops over at the Center, Jason does not show up. There is some estrangement between the two and Genesis no longer visits as much as he did because he feels betrayed by Nana Moira. Exactly what she feared. But there is nothing she can do about it because Jason is a grown man who is entitled to make his own decisions. Also, he is a positive presence at the Center.

In any event, Nana Moira feels Genesis should not be so pissed off with everyone because the boy still minds the cheese stall at the farmers' market for him on Saturdays, and even on some Wednesdays. Genesis, on the other hand, expected more than just minding a stall from his son. He wants him to learn the trade and be part of the family business. He thought Jason— whom he insists on calling Revelation—had returned from Yellow Springs precisely because the world had given him a few hard lessons about life, and that now he would be more serious and be an upright citizen; he would not be afraid to face his responsibilities like a man. Especially now that he has been baptized into the church of his ancestors who are known in history as hard workers who helped to build America into what it is today.

"But all he does is to sit here yap-yapping with the women," says Genesis on one of his visits to the Center.

"He don't only yap-yap," says Nana Moira. "He helps a lot here. And he's learning plenty of stuff."

"What can anyone learn yap-yapping with women?"

"What can anyone learn from women? You talk like you didn't come from a vagina."

This disarms Genesis and he breaks out laughing.

"I didn't," he says. "Caesarean."

"Same difference. You lived in some woman's innards."

The quilting women are scandalized. People don't call things like that by their names in these parts. Plus Genesis is too young to be talking such stuff with Nana Moira. He could easily be the age of Rachel's late pops. But he is enjoying the exchange with Nana Moira and even forgets that he is angry with his son.

The original reason Jason took up the volunteer offer was that he was going to be closer to Rachel. He hoped this would give them the opportunity to rehearse and busk together. But now he genuinely loves working here and enjoys the company—not only of the regular quilters but also of a variety of people from Jensen Township and from neighboring townships such as Rome, Ames, Dover, and Canaan. Sometimes storytellers descend from the hills and come out of the Wayne Forest to enjoy Nana Moira's special-occasion dinners and tell their tall tales to the joy of everyone, and to Nana Moira's cackling laughter. Special occasions are not only limited to Thanksgiving or Fourth of July or Valentine's Day. Nana Moira has a knack of coming up with a special occasion from the top of her head and starts cooking. Sometimes it is something that people can recognize, such as St. Patrick's Day or

Mother's Day, but at other times it is an obscure anniversary—the first time she had set her eyes on Robbie Boucher, for instance.

It bothers Jason that Rachel is usually somewhere else instead of enjoying his company at the Jensen Community Center. But he is biding his time. She will learn to appreciate him. And together they will create beautiful sounds that will haunt her soul and make her dream of him in the middle of the night as she sleeps in her room.

Fridays are his blissful moments because that's when she bakes bread to sell at the farmers' market the following day. She spends the whole day in the kitchen at the Center, and he helps her knead the dough, or he runs some errands to town in case she needs some more hickory nuts or flour or whatever else she uses in her recipes. They talk about the old days and laugh a lot. And they promise each other that soon they will start rehearsing and playing together. They giggle and guffaw and tease each other and chase each other around the tables and use the kitchen stools and lids of pots as shields when they blast each other with flour. Then they clean up the mess quickly before Nana Moira discovers it.

Nana Moira always keeps out of the kitchen on those days. She has indeed taken a shine on Jason, and she tells her granddaughter so one day. "I hope Sweet

Jesus will open your eyes one day and you'll see that this is a good man He has delivered right to your doorstep."

But Rachel has many other interests and, according to Nana Moira, takes Jason for granted. If she is not out there doing Appalachia Active stuff such as demonstrating at the Ohio Department of Natural Resources offices on East State Street to stop a well on the land of Mrs. Mayle, an eighty-four-year-old in Rome Township who does not want it on her property, she is visiting Schuyler—that crippled Schuyler, according to Nana Moira—and driving her to physiotherapy or to her community-service work at a nursing home in the city.

On Fridays when the baking resumes, Rachel does seem to reciprocate Jason's romantic—some may say amorous—attention. At least that's what he thinks. That's what Nana Moira thinks too, and she is ecstatic about it while it lasts. That's what the gossiping women of the Jensen Township Quilting Circle think as well, and they ask themselves behind Nana Moira's back why good things always fall on the laps of those who do not deserve them, those who fail to appreciate them.

One weekend Rachel goes to the Action Camp where she meets Skye Riley and things happen.

The camp is held in Stewart at an old building that used to be a school but now is used for varied community purposes. Different workshop sessions are going on at the same time in the classrooms, and Skye takes the initiative to look for Rachel until he finds her at the "Fracking 101 Workshop" where participants are learning how gas is extracted using horizontal hydraulic drilling technology. The content is of a much greater depth than at the Arts West meeting. From then on he is with her that whole day, accompanying her even to sessions he would not have attended otherwise; he has heard it all and seen it all.

Rachel is grateful for his company. She would have been quite lonely here without Schuyler; most of the participants are much older. Skye is with her when she attends the session on "Injection Wells" where they explore what happens to all the toxic frack waste, the dangers of injection wells and how Ohio has become a dumping ground for the waste. Just to be with her he even attends those sessions that deal with topics he detests, such as one on "Exhausting Administrative Remedies" where Rachel and the other participants learn what bases to cover before resorting to direct action. Skye tells Rachel during the lunch break that it was a session of appeasement, just like the one titled "Strategic Legal Defense" which explored ways to use court cases to further campaign goals.

"We are tired of playing by the rules of the establishment," says Skye, using a term that was fashionable in the heyday of demonstrations and sit-ins in those giddy years that baby-boomers like to boast about.

Skye is in his element when he facilitates his own workshop on "Strategic Direct Action." He makes the session great fun by letting participants play games and role-act scenarios based on his own experiences in West Virginia. "The cops can be a real drag," he says, and teaches the workshop what to expect from law enforcement and how to de-escalate dangerous situations. All the while his emphasis is on defiance action.

"They can't arrest us all," he says. "They can't kill all of us."

At first Rachel is a bit shy to make a fool of herself playing some of the games in front of Skye Riley. But soon she gets into the spirit of things, especially when Skye himself is leading the activities with abandon, becoming the life of the party in the process. Soon the workshop is raucous; even senior citizens are laughing themselves silly.

"When you're faced with real law enforcement you'll remember this moment and you'll know what to do," he says after all the horsing around.

After dinner of pizza delivered to the camp venue by a local restaurant, a movie is screened in the old school hall. But Rachel and Skye decide to skip it.

Instead they repair to Skye's motel room in the out-skirts of Athens, and there she sits on his bed and strums the guitar and sings "The Cuckoo," a favorite song that she once heard Jean Ritchie, the legendary balladeer from the hills of Kentucky, play so beautifully on her dulcimer.

He likes the guitar, and he says so.

"Only the guitar? I just sang you a song and you like only the guitar?" asks a wounded Rachel.

Skye Riley comes from the Blue Ridge Mountains where women sing of coal-mine accidents in gravelly voices, and where songs have been liberated from the tyranny of meter but are laden with ornaments. He cannot pretend he loves what he heard even if that becomes a deal breaker. He searches for kinder words in his head, but they don't exist.

"There's no voice that you can't do nothing about," he says. "Somebody can train you how to use yours to full effect. Back on the Blue Ridge Mountains I know some old singers who can shape it for you. You can be that whiny kind of singer that people love nonetheless."

She feels insulted. No one's ever told her she sucks.

"Did I hear you right? Did you just call me whiny?"

"In a good way," says Skye. "Almost yodelly. It can be a charming style of singing. All you need is to try to be nothing other than a whiny singer. You should appreciate the whine and use it to your advantage."

His honesty is so disarming that she breaks out laughing.

That night Rachel does not go home. And the following nights too; even though the Action Camp is over and the rest of the activists are back with their families.

When Jason sees her a week later he knows immediately that something happened at that camp. Rachel is withdrawn at the kitchen as they bake the bread. No fooling around. She is more intense than ever before. More focused. But when she is with Nana Moira and the quilting women she is relaxed and even bubbly. She is nicer to her grandma and stops complaining about her candy. One afternoon she even brings her Hershey's Kisses and places the box on Nana Moira's lap.

"There—but don't overdo it," she says.

She is chirpy in a way that makes those who know her uncomfortable.

"She needs to see a doctor," Nana Moira declares.

No one suspects that whatever happened at that camp has to do with a scrawny coal miner called Skye Riley. But no one has the time to dwell on Rachel's change of mood. Nana Moira is preoccupied with the new project that Jason is introducing to the Center.

After noticing the amount of waste that at his home would have been used for compost, Jason suggests that instead of dumping potato peels, onion skins, outer lettuce leaves, leftover food, and even scraps of non-recyclable paper in the garbage to end up in a landfill somewhere, they should build a compost heap.

"And do what with it? We don't keep a garden here," says Nana Moira.

"Maybe we should," says Jason.

"Am not keeping a garden, Jason. Am too old for that."

"You ain't gonna work on it yourself, Nana Moira."

Volunteers like him will look after the garden. After all, there are all these people who come to the Center to eat for free. Or just to sit on the porch and gossip about things that are none of their business. They could water the garden. Instead of depending solely on cabbages and Swiss chard from the Food Bank in Logan, Nana Moira could cook some real fresh vegetables for her guests.

"And you can even join the Compost Exchange too," says Jason. "Pa can tell you all about it 'cause he's one of the founders."

Nana Moira learns that she doesn't even need to have her own compost in the yard at the Center if she thinks that would be too much for her. All she needs is to join the Compost Exchange. They give you five-gallon buckets that you fill with the waste and then seal them off. You either take them to their booth at the farmers' market or they collect them from your premises if you are a business that produces a lot of waste, such as a restaurant. Each time you bring your bucket, they give you a clean, empty one. There is so much waste at the Center that Jason is certain the Compost Exchange folks would come and collect it. Every six months, members receive a five-gallon bucket of healthy compost for their own gardens.

"That way you get to be green major, Nana Moira," says Jason. "Pa says all this global warming stuff is because of them landfills. They pollute groundwater too. You become green, Nana Moira, if you don't dump stuff but compost it."

Nana Moira is sold on the idea. The backyard is big enough; the Center will have its own garden. It need not be large at first while everyone is learning. It will grow as they get more confident.

3

The weather has driven most of the traders into the mall. Their tables line up against the walls, forming a corridor from the entrance to the sofas in front of the department store, Elder-Beerman, where coffee-sipping townsfolk are lounging. The farmers' market is not really like the farmers' market when it is indoors, but even hardened men and women of the countryside don't want to risk frostbite from temperatures at fifteen degrees below freezing.

Jason stands behind a table laden with Genesis's aged cheese. Giving his dad a hand at mongering his produce is the least he can do since rebelling against working at the family's husbandry. The tables on his row and on the opposite one are heaving with winter squash, pasture-raised poultry and eggs, homemade candy of different fruit flavors, honey, beeswax candles, and bottles of apple sauce, apple cider, and apple vinegar that the women have made in their kitchens. There are also freezers behind some of the tables with Angus beefsteaks and roast, and lamb chops and legs—all grass-fed, lean, and without hormones, according to the scrawls hanging at the tables. Jason's only competition is the woman selling "grass-fed organic cheese." It is priced much lower than his because it is not aged.

The place was quite crowded in the morning but now the customers are beginning to thin out a bit. Every time someone opens the glass doors entering or exiting the mall, Jason cannot help taking a quick glance before returning his attention to a customer. Rachel should have been here by now. She is late on this—their first day of performing together. Maybe she wants to bail on him. He wouldn't be surprised if she did. There's always been some reticence on her part about this enterprise. Or maybe he is just being inse-cure. If only he could stop the butterflies fluttering like crazy in his stomach this whole morning. As if he has never performed before. He reminds himself that he is Jason de Klerk and he has performed with the likes of Big Flake Thomas, not only in the artsy streets of Yellow Springs but at the Chindo in front of crowds that were not apt to swallow any crap. He has always acquitted himself well. Once he and his didgeridoo even received a standing ovation playing at the park. Granted most people were already standing even before he began playing. But some of those who were sitting on the grass and on the benches stood up to applaud after some particularly deep and somber drones that reverberated down his instrument into the air.

But where the hell is Rachel?

The duo's debut should have happened three weeks ago, but the weather had other ideas. Snow and freezing rain made the roads slippery for days. For two Saturdays the farmers' market was cancelled. But Jason continued to brave the treacherous county and township roads and worked his way from Rome Township to the Jensen Community Center.

Nana Moira insisted on keeping the Center open so that seniors could come for hot soup. She told Jason there was no need for him to show up for work lest his fingers and toes fell off, and he promised he'd take heed. But the next day he was there, reciting his version of Herodotus as plagiarized by the architects of the New York City General Post Office: "Ain't no snow or rain or heat or the dark night or sleet or slush or crappy township roads gonna keep me away from you, Nana Moira."

"That's a song right there," said Rachel. "Just needs a little bit of rhyme."

"You see a song everywhere," said Jason.

"Don't drag me into it," said Nana Moira. "Got nothing to do with Moira Boucher. It's all about Rachel."

Then she broke into her trademark laughter, spilling her coffee on the table in the process.

Rachel's cheeks turned rosy, which brought even greater hilarity on Nana Moira.

"I hate it when you say such things," said Rachel.

She is still laughing as she wipes the coffee with rags from the floor.

"What if Nana Moira is right?" asked Jason.

Thanks to the bad weather Rachel was trapped at the township. She dared not risk driving to Schuyler's. So she just stayed at home and watched television. Or she nursed her car to the Center to help her grandma. Because not many people ventured outside, not even for Nana Moira's soup, Jason and Rachel spent the day rehearsing.

The first day he came with his didgeridoo and tumbadora Nana Moira could not recognize him. Neither could Rachel when she finally came to the Center. He was clean-shaven, exposing his angular chin, and had cut his flaxen hair to a wavy quiff. Rachel gasped, but soon got control of herself and pretended she was not impressed by the new look.

"What have you done to your face?" she asked.

"Nothing. Just removed all the extra hair."

"You look different."

"Only different?"

"Are you fishing for a compliment?"

"I did it for the music," Jason said. "You can't play the didj good with a beard."

He explained that with a beard it is not easy to form the proper seal at the mouthpiece.

Rachel did not have the staying power at the rehearsal. Soon she got bored. Perhaps it was the music. She didn't feel it. The didgeridoo sounded nothing like music to her. Just deep bellowing sound that didn't seem to have any direction. It went all over the place. It didn't seem to combine well with her bluegrass guitar either. But Jason assured her it was as it should be. Sometimes he demanded that she take a detour from her rhythmic sounds and strum and pluck the strings at random. She tried this and the result horrified her.

"It has no order, Jason, no rhyme, no reason," she said. "It's like jazz. I don't play jazz, Jason. Jazz doesn't make sense to anyone."

"Not jazz, Rachel. I don't know nothing about jazz. It's the new sound we're inventing. Trust me, people gonna like it major."

"Well, I'm tired of practicing."

So, they took a walk in the forest. Everything was black or white. The trunks of trees were black against the whiteness of the snow. The black branches were laden with snow and ice; some bending almost to breaking point. Everything else was an impenetrable whiteness. Even those bits of the sky showing through the top branches were white. Rachel was struck by the utter silence, and the smell of freshness. Nothing of the sounds of the forest that she relished whenever she took a walk in it, which would be in the spring, summer, or fall, but never in winter. It seemed that snow and ice swallowed all the sounds and rendered the forest mute. The two could not hear even the sounds of their own footsteps.

Rachel wanted to say something, but Jason shushed her; when the forest is like this you must respect its silence. She wanted to tell him about Skye Riley. She had not seen him since she spent almost a week with him in a motel room. She would not reveal the part about the motel room. She would just tell Jason that something developed between them, and the guy never called or took the trouble to see her again. They texted each other, and all his texts were about how busy he was either working at the mine or organizing the workers and the communities against corporate greed. He wrote as if that week didn't happen between them, or if it did, it didn't mean as much to him as to her. And then the texts also stopped. She wanted to ask Jason what to do in a case like this. He being a guy would know what went on in the heads of guys. She had come to see Jason more and more as a brother and didn't imagine there would be anything wrong in discussing her longing for Skye Riley with him.

His thoughts, on the other hand, were at a different place. He had a burning desire for her. If only he could hold her in his arms, right there in that icy forest, and plaster her face with kisses. He dared not do that though. He was biding his time. She would come around. She had almost come around, until she became distant again after that damned Action Camp.

"How old is this cheese here?"

The customer's question brings Jason back to Genesis's aged cheese.

Rachel arrives towards midday and finds Jason sulking.

"My car wouldn't start," she says. "Had to wait for Nana Moira to jump-start it."

"You should have called me, Rachel. Like now most folks are gone. The farmers' market will close in an hour."

"We can do it. There're still some folks."

They repair to the lounge area and set up their busk station and start playing. He opens with the tumbadora, and then Rachel joins with the guitar. People stop and listen. Soon a small crowd has gathered around them. Jason reaches for the didgeridoo and droning sounds are echoed down the tube in relayed vibrations.

Sometimes he prolongs the drone, and then suddenly shouts into the instrument, making it growl and bark like a dog. To Rachel's surprise the audience enjoys these antics. It must be for the novelty, she concludes, not for the music. She feels superfluous with her guitar. All the eyes are on the didgeridoo, not on her.

Blue sits in the open guitar case as if guarding the change and a few greenbacks that are beginning to accumulate. Jason did not complain when Rachel placed her there. He knows that Blue is Rachel's mascot; she brings her luck. That's what she told him once when she was still busking alone and selling pawpaw bread when the fruit was still in season.

Jason is giving her the evil eye; she knows immediately that he is expecting more from her. She has been keeping to the fast but ordered tempo of her Appalachian tradition. She has to improvise. She feels silly as she flatpicks random notes and chords that don't make any sense to her, but that animate Jason to more drones and other sounds that mimic cooing doves and quacking ducks and bleating goats and neighing horses. All the while he is performing a dance that is made even more awkward by the weight and the length of the instrument. According to Rachel there is nothing musical about all these crazy sounds, but the crowd is all agape and laughing and clapping hands. Its attention continues to be solely on Jason, and this pisses her off.

"Never seen nothing like this," says a spectator.

"It's all this New Age stuff," responds another.

A woman pushes her way to the front, and between songs she yells, "Why do you have an Amish woman guarding filthy lucre?"

Rachel is jolted a bit, but she summons a friendly mien.

"This is Blue," she says. "Blue, meet the nice lady."

But the nice lady has no time for pleasantries.

"You making fun of Amish folks, making them sit with filthy lucre listening to this devilish music?"

Jason has no time for niceties. He yells back at the lady.

"No Amish sitting nowhere near here, ma'am. This is just a fuckin' doll."

"You think I'm stupid?" asks the lady, and then storms away down the corridor of organic produce. Spectators wonder why an Amish doll should bug her so much. She is not even Amish herself. Another one notes that maybe she hates to see folks who bite the hands that feed her; she sells lots of homemade noodles and jams that she buys from Amish country.

Rachel is too rattled to continue with the show. Why would anyone hate Blue? She has been busking with her ever since Nana Moira found her where she had hidden her, and no one has ever complained. Jason gives her a long tight hug, while assuring her that everything is fine, she shouldn't worry about the crazy woman. The closeness leaves his heart beating fast and gives him an unwelcome hard-on. He wishes this could happen every day; a whole gang of Amish women could terrify her into his arms.

An angry Genesis breaks the moment. He drove like a madman all the way from Rome Township, fourteen miles away, after he received a phone call from a neighboring stall that Jason had abandoned his cheese and was busy fooling around with a didgeridoo and a girl. And here he is, indeed, in the arms of a girl with the silly didgeridoo on the floor in front of them.

"I've lost many customers because of your irresponsibility," says Genesis, and he leads Jason back to the aged cheese table.

The farmers and sundry traders are already packing their goods away.

Rachel stands there for a while. Then she gathers the money and puts it in her bag. Blue is chucked into the same bag as well. Rachel packs her guitar in the case, and as she passes the cheese table she hears Genesis yell, "That Boucher girl leads you astray."

She knows those words were directed at her; Genesis wanted her to hear them. She stops for a while, waiting to hear if Jason has anything to say in her defense. But Jason does not defend her. He is sullenly packing the cheese away in its boxes.

Rachel wonders why Jason lets Genesis intimidate him. She'd never let Nana Moira bully her this way.

Jason spends most of the day splitting wood for Nana Moira. He has been at it for days and the pile is enough to last the whole winter. Maybe for the next winter as well. Or even for the next two winters. When he sets out to do something, he is relentless.

"It's enough, Jason. You don't need to kill yourself," Nana Moira told him this morning, as she did yesterday morning, and the morning before.

He never responds. He just keeps on swinging the maul and whistling and humming and breaking out into a song whose lyrics no one can follow. He is topless and his body is glistening with sweat. Nana Moira is beginning to worry about him. From time to time she picks up her walking stick and hobbles to the back of the building where the pile of wood is growing and asks him if everything is fine, and if he doesn't want to take a breather. He just shakes his head without stopping.

Towards midday, Nana Moira goes to the back of the building again, this time determined that she would not take "no" for an answer.

"Come for some soup, Jason," she says firmly.

"Might as well take a smoke break," he says, leaving the maul buried in a stump.

He takes one of the old car seats on the porch, and rolls himself a cigarette. The smell of tomato-and-basil soup wafts in his direction, reminding him that he has not had anything to eat today. He left home before his stepmom prepared breakfast.

It is one of those erratic winter days when the temperature shoot up to seventy. It is all because of global warming, the likes of Genesis who see themselves as the guardians of the environment will tell you. But to Nana Moira, only ninnies would complain about a nice day like this. Give it whatever name you like, and attribute its beauty to anything you fancy, it is a day not to be wasted indoors. So she is sitting on an old car seat at the porch with two senior citizens who are regulars at the Center.

Rachel drives into the yard in her Ford Escort. Even as she walks out of the car to join them Nana Moira stands up and bows in mock reverence.

"Sweet Jesus, am just stumped what we did right to deserve the pleasure of Miss Rachel's company on a nice day like this," she says in a hoity-toity voice.

"Sarcasm doesn't make you beautiful, Nana Moira," says Rachel.

"Before you sit down, get Jason some soup."

"And some bread too," adds Jason.

Rachel goes to the kitchen.

Nana Moira's hands cannot stay idle; she is hand-stitching together pieces cut from old dresses. They will become batting for a quilt.

Rachel returns with a cup of tomato-and-basil soup and two slices of bread on a side plate. She places them on the floor in front of Jason's seat.

"We gonna practice this afternoon. That's why Rachel is here," says Jason helpfully.

"As if I need a reason to be at my grandma's work-place," says Rachel.

"Ha! So Jason's horn wins over Schuyler?" says Nana Moira.

"That sounds rude, Nana Moira," says one of the senior citizens. The implications of her statement dawn on her, and she breaks out cackling. The two seniors join her, and between the bouts of guffaws they exclaim how irrepressible Nana Moira is. Both Jason and Rachel do not see anything funny. Jason wonders why his didgeridoo should be the cause of such mirth, while Rachel is quite flustered after finally catching their drift.

"You're all old for nothing," she says, and walks into the building.

But she is soon brought back by a roar that is so loud it shakes the walls. And there entering the yard is the scrawny figure of Skye Riley perched on a monstrous bike. On the rear fender is a tall cycle-flagpole on which flies a huge American flag. He parks next to Nana Moira's GMC Suburban and revs the engine a few times to impress the onlookers at the porch. Jason cannot but stand in awe.

"That's a lot of bike," he says.

"'Cause he's a lot of man," says Rachel.

"He looks nothing like a lot of man to me," says Nana Moira. "He's too skinny like his mama never fed him nothing when he was a baby."

"Like they say, Nana Moira, it's what is inside that counts. He may be skinny to you, but he's a lot of man inside."

Skye walks to the porch with a big grin and a hand outstretched in what he sees as a friendly gesture. He vigorously shakes the hands of the two senior citizens, and then of Nana Moira's.

"You must be Nana Moira," he says. "Rachel told me so much about you."

"This is Skye Riley, my friend," says Rachel.

"Why don't you say it like it is: boyfriend," says Jason.

"You're right, my man," says Skye as he shakes Jason's hand. Then he grabs Rachel and kisses her. She pushes him away.

"That's a lot of bike you have there, buddy," says one of the seniors.

"Thanks. It's a Honda Valkyrie."

"Skye is a mineworker," says Rachel, as if that explains the bike, "from West Virginia."

"I'd rather be seen on a Harley Davidson," says Jason, displaying as much contempt on his face as he can muster. "It's a man's bike, and it's American too. What's the point of flying an American flag on a foreign bike?"

"Different strokes, buddy," says Skye smiling at him patronizingly and patting him on the shoulder.

"What's foreign about a beautiful bike like that?" asks one of the seniors.

"Its name. Honda. It's made by them Chinese," says Jason.

"Japanese," says Skye.

"Same difference," says Jason.

"I fought at Pearl Harbor," says the senior.

"Nobody fought in Pearl Harbor, gramps," says Skye. "The Japanese bombed the daylights out of us and killed thousands of our men."

"I don't like your boyfriend, Rachel," says the senior with urgency.

"He knows too much," adds the second senior.

Then everyone is sullen. Except Skye and Rachel. He is puzzled because he had no intention of rubbing anyone the wrong way. She is abashed. Nana Moira decided at the very introduction, and on hearing that the scrawny man was Rachel's boyfriend, that he was not worth her time. She is focusing on her sewing and on humming some random notes that are meant to inform Skye: "I am ignoring you, in case you didn't notice."

After some brief awkwardness Skye says, "Hey Rache, you need to come over with me to the Blue Ridge Mountains. Rain found us a balladeer who's gonna help you work on your voice till you can sing like our mountain women."

"Who's Rain?"

"My sister. She's a balladeer too, known and loved from the Blue Ridge Mountains to the hills of Kentucky. In all the tri-state area, they talk of Rain."

Jason cannot contain himself. He struts around and stands right in front of Skye.

"Rachel don't need to work on nothing with no one on the Blue Ridge Mountains. We making good money playing right here in Athens."

"Tell your friend to get out of my face, Rachel."

"Jason, please." And then she turns to Skye and tells him she is not interested in working with anyone in

West Virginia, and that Skye has some nerve to disappear for weeks on end, then come out of the blue and think that she's just going to leave everything and run after him.

"You're mad at me 'cause you don't know what I've been through," says Skye. "Let me take you for a ride and I'm gonna tell you all about it."

"He's taking you for a ride alright," says Nana Moira.

Rachel is wary of the pillion. She remembers what happened to Schuyler. But she really wants to hear what Skye has to say. She is eager to confirm what she has been trying to convince herself all these weeks— that Skye would not just disappear like that without a good reason, not after spending the kind of a steamy week she had never spent with any man before. Also, she is getting annoyed by Nana Moira's attitude toward her guest, and by everyone else's. To spite them, she jumps on to the pillion.

As the bike thunders away, Nana Moira yells after her granddaughter: "You ride the darn thing without a helmet, don't come crying to me when your brains are splattered all over the pavement."

All eyes are on Jason. He hates it when people feel sorry for him. He snaps at the three seniors: "What?" and then goes back to splitting wood.

Nana Moira is worried that he may hurt himself because she can hear him splitting with a vengeance that borders on recklessness.

"She's been taking lessons from that floozy, Schuyler," Nana Moira finally says after contemplating her granddaughter's behavior.

"Don't get too worried, Nana Moira," says one of the seniors. "At least the boy's got money. He's gonna take good care of her."

Nana Moira used to resent it when people her age, or even older, called her "nana," taking their cue from Rachel when she was a toddler. But she learned to accept it; although occasionally, like now, it jolts her a bit.

"It's all flash money," says Nana Moira dismissively. "A man should work for foundation money instead, so as to set up a family."

"Yep," agrees the senior. "All flash money. Cruising around like he owns Jensen."

The seniors are silent for a while. Nana Moira is sewing away. One of the men opens a Skoal Long Cut, takes out a few strings and places them between the cheeks and the gum. He passes it to the next man who places the tobacco between his upper lip and the gum. They both start chewing rhythmically. They close their eyes as they savor the flavor. And then they spit out a black jet in unison. It splatters way clear off the porch on the paved parking space in front of the building. They applaud; they are in their eighties, but they pride themselves in the power of their mouths; they can beat men half their age in any spitting competition. Nana Moira just keeps on sewing as if nothing is happening around her.

And then all of a sudden she bursts out: "A mineworker shouldn't be so skinny. His muscles gotta ripple like a lake when you drop a pebble. Like Jason's."

Jason hears none of this praise. He is behind the building swinging away, the mountain of wood growing in front of him.

The two men decide in unison that it is much safer not to contribute their opinion on the matter. Instead, they take refuge in their Skoal and chew and spit away to their hearts' content. Nana Moira focuses on her sewing.

"That boy's gonna hurt her so bad she won't know what hit her," says Nana Moira after a long silence. The seniors respond only by chewing even more furiously, and then ejecting another black jet. One grunts his pleasure, the other sneezes. No one blesses anyone. Another long silence follows.

"Who's gonna stop her if she wanna be a biker-bitch?" Nana Moira breaks the peace again.

Rachel, however, does not see herself in the light of a tough-acting broad, riding on the back of a bike, and being anarchic all over the place. She is sitting under a tree in the Wayne Forest, demanding answers from her beau. They have a small picnic pack of hot dogs and soda between them.

He was in a mine accident, he tells Rachel. He was taken out unconscious on a gurney and spent ten days in hospital after a cable snapped, sending coal-laden carts whirling uncontrollably. The last thing he remembers was when he pushed workers out of the way, saving a number of them. Only three, including him, were injured. It could have been worse if he did not have the presence of mind to act quickly.

Rachel feels bad for thinking the worst of a hero who had saved his fellow workers from certain death! But still she wants to know why he didn't call her or even text when he had gained consciousness at the hospital.

"I didn't want to bother you with my personal problems," he says. "You guys are involved in a big task here of trying to stop fracking. My personal issues count for nothing."

Then he goes on about the struggle against fracking companies, and how the people shall finally be victorious. He talks about demonstrations and sit-ins that are planned, of the heroes, mostly women, who have been chaining themselves to equipment and have been arrested. He expresses his wish that one day Rachel will be one of those heroes.

Rachel would rather be talking about their relationship and where it is going, but there is no stopping Skye Riley when he is on about direct action.

"I am scared for you," says Rachel after forcing a word in edgeways. "Your job is dangerous. Ever thought of doing something else?"

Skye looks at her as if she has uttered the dumbest statement ever.

"I am a coal miner, Rachel. It is what I do. The men who work in the coal mines will tell you that they wouldn't do anything else. It is our life. All our relatives for generations have worked in the coal mines. My grandfather was a coal miner, so was my father. My uncles are coal miners. I grew up playing hide-and-seek in abandoned mines. It is my life. So don't be scared for me. You should be scared for your people instead."

He goes into a tirade about how her people are in danger because of the skullduggery of fracking companies. They have new ways of spreading their poison in poor communities, as they are planning to do in Jensen Township. He lectures her as if she is in a classroom. Brine, he says, can be disposed on roads in Ohio legally—all the companies need is a resolution from the city council, the county commissioners, or even the township trustees to allow this to happen. In Jensen Township they plan to pass such a resolution. The township trustees will be taking such a vote at their next meeting.

This is news to Rachel. She is more surprised that Skye, all the way from West Virginia, even knows the days the trustees of Jensen meet at the Township House—the last Tuesday of every month at 5:30 p.m. The township will get some money if it allows brine to be spread on its roads, and this will offset some budget cuts. Rachel remembers vaguely hearing some Center regulars gossiping about the township fiscal officer who was under fire for some bookkeeping errors. Maybe that's part of the desperation that has led the township trustees to take such a drastic step at the expense of the health of the citizens.

"They have been lied to," says Skye. "The companies have given them facts and figures that show that a little brine on township roads is harmless."

Rachel is no longer listening. She is clearing the litter from their picnic spot and stuffing it in a plastic bag, making as much rustling and crunching noise as possible.

"You're right to be annoyed," says Skye. "This is happening right here in your township. You should have been vigilant. You should have been the one who alerts Appalachia Active instead of me from the Blue Ridge Mountains."

"Is this how it will be, Skye? It will be about the people all the time?"

"That's what we're here for, isn't it?"

"It's got to be about us sometimes."

It dawns on him that he got carried away. He has been told of his one-track mind, and he can kick himself for it.

"About us, eh? You're right—it has to be about us."

He leads her to the bike, and they thunder away.

It's late in the afternoon when they return to the Center. The first thing that Rachel notices is that Nana Moira's car is gone but Jason's is still parked on the driveway, next to Rachel's. She is, of course, not aware that Nana Moira went home early today to sleep off the pain that she caused her. Jason, on the other hand, is still splitting wood. He is struggling with a piece of wood that has a crotch in it. He uses a steel wedge to split it parallel to the plane of the crotch. The wedge flies out and leaves a point of attachment between the halves.

Rachel and Skye can hear the sound of the maul as they walk into the building. He doesn't give it a second thought; she wonders at his obsessive behavior.

Nana Moira did not lock up because Rachel's car keys are still in her coat where she left it on the chair. Before she left she asked Jason to remind Rachel to lock up if she returned while he was still at the Center.

"I'll wait till she returns," he promised her.

He hears the roar of the showy motorcycle and believes that Skye will just drop Rachel and then ride away. As soon as Skye leaves he will talk to Rachel before she drives home. That's what he was waiting for. To talk to Rachel. She's got to know how he feels, what her tomfoolery with Skye is doing to him and to Nana Moira and to everyone else who loves her.

All of five minutes are gone but Jason does not hear the Honda rumbling away. He gives the wood one more whack and then buries the maul in the stump. He dons his T-shirt and then his hoodie and walks to the building. The motorcycle is parked in front of the door, its metallic maroon finish glistening in the light from the window.

It is through the same window that he sees Skye chasing Rachel around the quilting tables. She is laughing and screeching all over the place. With her long strides she is faster than him. He grabs one of Nana Moira's unfinished quilts and throws it at her like a cowboy trying to lasso a cow. But she ducks and the quilt drops on the floor. Jason is fuming inside—how dare they treat Nana Moira's work of art with such disrespect?

Jason has seen this fooling around before. He used to do it with Rachel in the kitchen during those halcyon Fridays when they baked pawpaw bread.

Skye pretends he is giving up. He is out of breath and takes a seat. Rachel is off her guard as she walks too close to him. All of a sudden he leaps up and grabs her screeching and kicking. He plants a kiss on her lips. She melts in his arms. Soon they are stripping each other's clothes off. Reckless passion has overcome them and they cannot rip them off fast enough. Soon they are completely naked and rolling on Nana Moira's unfinished quilt on the floor.

Jason is livid and aroused as he listens to the moans. He was chopping wood the whole day, now he is chopping it in other ways. They come together in a crescendo of three tortured voices.

4

Jason has taken to mopping the floor at the Center incessantly. He used to mop it once a week without being asked. And this was welcomed by Nana Moira because no one bothered to mop the floor except when the Center was expecting prospective donors. Even for special-occasion lunches and dinners, the floor was swept but rarely mopped. Until Jason joined the Center. But lately he mops every day. The first thing he does when he arrives in the morning is mop the floor with bleached water, and the last thing he does before leaving for Rome Township in the afternoon is mop with a foamy detergent.

"This is no hospital, Jason," Nana Moira said on one occasion after she had gotten tired of shifting her chair from one spot to another. "I don't wanna be living in a sanitized place."

Sometimes members of the Quilting Circle would be sitting at their tables sewing away and laughing at their own jokes, and Jason would suddenly reach for the bucket, the mop, the detergent. He would scrub one particular area on the floor with so much force it bordered on violence. As if he was fighting a stubborn spot that was refusing to be removed. None of the women could understand why he had this expression of anger on his face.

Even today, on Christmas Eve, Jason is mopping the floor. It is rather annoying to Nana Moira because he is on the way of people who are preparing the place for the Christmas party in the evening. The Center is buzzing with community volunteers dressing up the Christmas tree with illuminated ornaments, hanging streamers and period posters of square dancers on the walls, and arranging the tables on the sides to make a dance space in the middle.

"You don't need to fight the floor, Jason," Nana Moira says.

"Just cleaning, Nana Moira. Just wanna keep the place spotless major, it being Christmas and all."

Nana Moira can only shake her head and move on to the kitchen to attend to her pies in the oven.

"Come over here give me a hand, Jason," she says from the kitchen.

It is the only way to get him off the mop and out of the way. In a few hours the kids will be here to build their gingerbread houses, and then the party will begin, first for the kids, then later in the evening, for the adults.

Jason gives the invisible spot a last wipe, and then puts the mop and the bucket away. He joins Nana Moira in the kitchen. She is preparing eggnog. She mumbles that most of this work should have been done days before, but people don't want to help. All they want is to eat when someone else has prepared the fixings. Even her own Rachel would rather be helping strangers, such as driving Schuyler all over the place like she is her servant, instead of giving her grandma a hand at the Center. Only Genesis's boy has been by her side. Only Sweet Jesus knows how she would cope without Genesis's boy.

"Come on, Nana Moira," says Jason, "you done fine long before I came here."

She is beating eggs, sugar, and salt in a large pot and asks Jason to slowly pour the milk into the mix as she is whisking. After that Jason places the pot on the burner, while Nana Moira makes certain that the stove has a very low heat setting.

"Just keep on stirring until it thickens, Jason," says Nana Moira. "Then we'll add vanilla extract and nutmeg."

This will be the non-alcoholic version of eggnog that the kids will enjoy. While it heats on the stove where it will remain at least for an hour, with Jason stirring it occasionally, they set out to create another eggnog masterpiece, but this time with alcohol. In a large punch bowl, they combine the mixture with bourbon, rum, and brandy. There is some left in each of the three bottles, so Nana Moira gives it to Jason with the warning: "Don't get wasted."

Jason hides the bottles in the cupboard, behind some pots.

"I've folks that hail from Chester Hill that'll be playing music tonight. You and Rachel will play too, won't you? High time I hear the silly music folks tell me you play."

"Me and Rachel gonna play nothing, Nana Moira."

Nana Moira has been aware for some time now that a new coldness has developed between Jason and Rachel. Well, maybe not coldness, but some distance. Some falling out of sorts, though no one's talked about it. It began that afternoon, the only time that Nana Moira set her eyes on that damned Skye Riley. She suspects that her granddaughter has been so taken up by the scrawny coal miner from West Virginia that she is spurning the only great thing that ever happened to her—namely, Jason de Klerk. Of course, she's not aware that the estrangement comes from Jason's side. On the now-rare occasions that Rachel comes to the Center, Jason refuses to talk to her. When she walks in he walks out, gets into his car, and drives away. Every time he looks at her he sees Skye Riley buried between her thighs.

Rachel, on the other hand, has stayed away from the Center for different reasons, though they also have to do with Skye. Ever since he told her about the Jensen Township Board of Trustees' impending vote on allowing fracking companies to cover township roads with brine, she has been animated to action. She organized a few members of Appalachia Active who come from Jensen and neighboring townships, and they mill around the Township Building on County Road 9889 holding placards with huge skulls and chanting slogans. But Rachel has taken her protest to another level. Whereas the rest of the protesters only gather on the days when the trustees will be meeting or will be having consultations with the residents, she goes there every day and stands outside the building all alone with a placard scrawled: *No Poisonous Brine on Jensen Roads*. Her one-woman demonstrations have become the talk of the township. The first Nana Moira heard of them was from the women of the Quilting Circle. She was hurt to discover that Rachel was doing things out there that people knew about, and yet she was ignorant of them. A chasm was growing between her and her granddaughter, and soon it would be too wide to bridge. That evening she tried to speak with Rachel about it, but she was uncommunicative. Nana Moira lost her temper and yelled at her.

"It's that Skye Riley, isn't it? You just trying to impress him."

She knew she was right when Rachel told her it was none of her business.

It is true that Rachel hoped Skye Riley would be proud of her. Members of Appalachia Active were sure to report her dedication to the cause to him. Maybe if he heard she cared just as much as he does for "the people," he would be more attentive to her desires—particularly the singular desire to spend time with him like normal people who are in a relationship. The last time she saw him was when he came thundering on a bike and left in the evening after a roll in the hay—except the hay was Nana Moira's unfinished quilt. It's been weeks since then. They texted each other for a few days. But the texts dwindled off as the days went by. He would see her, he kept on promising. He missed her, he assured her. He was held up by the work at the mine, or by the demonstrations and sit-ins, or by some time spent in a county jail waiting to be bailed out after inciting some mini-riot at a hydraulic fracturing plant or at a mountaintop removal mining site.

Surely her one-woman demonstration in Jensen Township would reach his ears on the distant Blue Ridge Mountains and he would come to her. She was aware that Jason was giving her the silent treatment, but she did not know that it was more than just that she left with Skye that day. Jason needed to understand and accept that she had made her choice.

"So why won't you and Rachel play tonight?" asks Nana Moira.

"We didn't rehearse nothing," says Jason. "We don't play together no more."

Nana Moira had not been aware that the estrangement had gone to such an extent. Jason tells her that he now busks alone every Saturday at the farmers' market. In any event their experiment with Rachel did not work. She was too bent on playing the music of her fathers and grandfathers while he wanted to dabble in experimental sounds. She was often late for performances, and sometimes did not rehearse, mostly because she was attending Appalachia Active meetings and demonstrations, or was driving Schuyler to physio. He complained, he begged, he threatened. Rachel promised that the following week she would be on time and during the week she would make time to rehearse, but things never went down that way. And then Skye Riley came out of the blue and everything changed.

Now he plays his didgeridoo alone. He has even done away with the tumbadora. Just the man and his didj without any frills. And people love it. He draws better crowds than he did when he was with Rachel and is making more money. People are fascinated by the deep drone of the instrument, and the various tones he is able to muster all at once. He never fails to get applause and requests for an encore whenever he produces vibrations and reverberations that seem to shake the very earth the people are standing on.

"You let Rachel run all over you," says Nana Moira.

"*You* let Rachel run all over you," says Jason.

"Give us a shot," says Nana Moira.

Jason gets the bottle of bourbon from behind the pots and pours them a shot in paper cups.

"You shouldn't let Rachel get away with everything," says Nana Moira as she slugs the drink in one swig. "You gonna lose her to that skinny West Virginia boy."

"You lose nothing you never owned in the first place, Nana Moira."

"With that attitude you'll get nowhere. She's ripe for the plucking and you snoozing."

There is commotion in the quilting room. The kids have arrived. Jason is one of two judges in the gingerbread house competition, so he leaves Nana Moira to her cooking and baking. The place is buzzing as the moms and older sisters help the kids unpack kits of prebaked gingerbread houses from boxes. The kids are in groups of two or three, depending on their ages. Jason starts the stopwatch. The winning group is the one that will have the best decorated house in thirty minutes. The room fills with the aromas of confection. Walls are erected and cemented together with icing.

Then the roofs, the doors, the windows. Some kids use Hershey bars for the doors and gelatin sheets for almost clear windows. More icing on the roof for snow. The more creative ones use shredded wheat cereal on the roofs or colorful cookies layered as shingles. M&Ms, Skittles, and candy corn make the walls and the roofs colorful. Some are even used to fence the houses. Shredded coconut or just sugar spread in front of the houses become snow on which gingerbread Santas mingle with naked gingerbread men. Some houses are wobbly and cannot stand the weight of the decorations. They come tumbling down and the owners burst into tears. Jason has to cast off his role as a judge and become a comforter and consoler.

Nana Moira watches from the kitchen entrance. She smiles to herself and says under her breath, "He would be very good with my great-grandchildren."

Savory scents of baking pies wafting from the kitchen mingle with the minty and gingerly aromas that fill the quilting room.

The only compensation for the sad fact that it won't be a white Christmas again this year is that the kids can make a bonfire outside and roast marshmallows.

A dinner of savory and sweet pies was had by all, and a lot of soda and eggnog was quaffed. Toys donated

by the Athens business community and sundry philan-
thropists were handed out by a doddering Santa who
would have fallen to pieces if any of the kids had sat
on his lap. The infants and toddlers have been taken
home to bed, and the quilting room has become a
dance hall. A bluegrass trio from Chester Hill is singing
and playing the mandolin, banjo, and dulcimer. It is a
square dance theme party and most of the younger
women are resplendent in fancy dresses with rows of
ruffles, lace, and ribbons. Some are in color-coordinated
ruffled dresses, petticoats, and even pettipants. Most of
the men are in their sloppy everyday plaid shirts and
denim jeans. But two or three fops are in long-sleeved
country-and-western shirts with bolo ties, neat jeans,
cowboy hats, and boots with taps.

In these early hours of the dance only one or two
couples are dancing. The rest are standing in groups
talking and laughing and drinking punch or eggnog.
Genesis and his wife are cracking a few jokes with
Nana Moira. The wife is properly attired, while Genesis
is in his old, hippie tie-dye tee and faded jeans. Nana
Moira is in a bright blue Prairie skirt, albeit a long one.
She takes this dance seriously and admonishes Genesis.
She says she expected better from him, but it turns out
he is no different from the other men who have lost
respect for tradition and culture and come to the
square dance dressed any which way. Thanks to the
spoilsports it is not quite the fifties theme party she

had hoped this would be. Although she had not announced it that way, all this effort was in memory of Robbie Boucher. Sadly, the men failed to live up to that memory.

"But it makes no never mind," she says after giving Genesis a few more choice words, and gently admonishing his wife for not getting him in line, "square dance is square dance even when some folks are disrespectful."

Jason, who still has the habit of avoiding his father when he is at the Center though he still lives in his house, is on one of the car seats on the porch, watching the kids using long sticks as skewers to roast marshmallows. A curious boy walks over to him.

"What's up, Jase?"

"Get your ass outta here!" growls Jason.

The boy is taken aback. Was this not the guy who was laughing and cracking jokes at the gingerbread-house competition? He scampers away to join his buddies at the fireside.

Jason does not want any kid bothering him because he is involved in very serious business—he is creating sizzurp in a soda bottle. He is mixing Phernegan—a brand of cough syrup that has large amounts of promethazine and codeine—with Mountain Dew and pieces of Jolly Rancher candy. He uses a Styrofoam cup to drink the mixture, and soon he feels all fuzzy inside and regrets why he was rude to the boy.

He calls him to come and join him, but the boy yells back: "Fuck you!"

He is attacked by so much happiness he wants to cry. He stands and dances to the music from the quilting room. The headlights of a car shine on him as it drives into the yard. He dances even more vigorously for the light. The parking space in front of the building is chock-full—some space where cars would normally be parked is taken up by the bonfire—so the car reverses and parks outside the fence. Rachel and Schuyler get out of the car and walk into the yard. Immediately Jason sees them and shouts excitedly, waving his hands, "Hey Schuyler! Hey Rache!"

"I thought you said he was not talking to you," says Schuyler to Rachel.

"He was not," says Rachel.

"Come join me, girls," says Jason. "Rache, you pretty Santy Claus you!"

She does look very beautiful in black knee-high boots and a three-piece Santa costume—a teeny-weeny, itsy-bitsy red miniskirt and hood, both with white faux fur trim, and a black-and-red velvet top. She is not wearing any coat despite the cold; she left it in the car to show off her attire. Schuyler does not look bad herself, though showing less flesh in a black pantsuit and a down jacket with a hood. She still hobbles on her single crutch.

"What's up, Jason?" says Schuyler, when they get to him.

"Try this," he says, giving Rachel the Styrofoam cup. In his euphoria, he has forgotten he is not talking to her. He loves everybody and he wants to share his sizzurp.

"What's this?" asks Rachel.

"Hey, that smells like slim," says Schuyler.

"What's slim?" asks Rachel.

"Slim, sizzurp, same difference," says Jason.

"You don't know slim? Been living under a rock lately, Rache? That's what the hip-hop guys call purple drank. That's why he's so happy. It does that to you."

"I'll have none of it. I'm on my own high," says Rachel as she walks away toward the door.

"Me neither," says Schuyler, hobbling after her. The women enter the building.

"Hey Rache!" Jason calls after them, giggling, "Where's Blue? How come you're here without Blue? I love Blue, Rache! She guards our money and it grows and grows, all because of fuckin' Blue."

He follows them into the quilting room and starts clogging alone like crazy. He is the only one who is clogging. The rest of the people have formed two circles of eight dancers each. They are gleeful as they do the flutterwheel, then reverse the flutter, and pass the ocean, all of which are square dance steps that leave the couples giggly and giddy. Rachel is dancing up a storm in one of the circles. So is Nana Moira who, to Rachel's surprise, does not need the walking stick when she dances. Of course her joints are stiff and arthritic and she dances like the old lady she is, but her dance partners are only too happy to support her and nurse her along. One can see that back in the day she used to be a nifty dancer. Genesis, particularly, relishes dancing with Nana Moira. Actually everyone wants to dance with Nana Moira. She is the celebrity of the night. Schuyler can only sit on the sidelines and watch.

Early in the morning, a few hours before dawn, Jason is driving Rachel's car back to the Jensen Community Center after dropping Schuyler at home in Rome Township. Rachel is dozing next to him. The crisp winter air outside penetrates the old Ford Escort and makes Jason alert. The events of the party return to him in incoherent snatches.

After his marathon clogging, the sizzurp wore off and he was in the dumps. He just sat there, next to Schuyler, and stared at the dancers. Occasionally Nana Moira joined them when she got tired. Jason was not responsive to their conversation. "That's what slim does to some people," said Schuyler. "You would know, wouldn't you?" said Nana Moira. She couldn't help being bitchy to Schuyler. It was no secret that she didn't like her one bit; she merely tolerated her for Rachel's sake.

Nana Moira didn't sit for long. Soon she was up and about serving potato and corn chips with dip and urging people to have some. Then she went back on the floor, dancing.

Jason steals a look at Rachel. Her head rests on his shoulder. He only has to tilt his head slightly to feel the silky hair against his cheeks. He drives very slowly. The bumpy road makes her head rub against his face. Occasionally she wakes up and tries to sit upright. But in no time she is dozing off again, giving him a thrill that he cannot prolong enough.

"There'll be a lot of cleaning up tomorrow," says Rachel as they enter the Center.

At the Center, paper plates and cups are strewn all over the place. Some of the ornaments have been stripped from the Christmas tree and form a trail to the door.

"And you won't be there for it," says Jason.

He takes a chair.

"Who says?"

"You're never there for nothing."

She sits on the table.

"You're not going to start on that again," she says. "Must go home now. Will sleep for the whole day."

He is rolling a joint.

"Okay, no sweat. Let's share a peace pipe. It's Christmas, Rachel. We don't wanna waste Christmas."

They share a spliff, although Rachel only takes two tokes.

"This'll pick us up," says Jason.

"It'll give us the munchies instead," says Rachel.

Jason goes to the kitchen and comes with slices of fruitcake on a paper plate. They start eating. She only has a slice, and he stuffs himself.

"We should lock up and go. Where are my car keys, Jase?" says Rachel.

He pats his pockets and says, "I must have left them in the car. I'll get them."

Instead of going to her car he goes to his. He gets a can of Old Spice from the glove compartment and sprays himself liberally. He returns to the quilting room. The scent of cologne is not lost on her. She suspects this is some feeble attempt at seduction and chuckles to herself.

"The keys?" she asks.

"Come on, Rache, we still having a great time. Tell you what, I got some bourbon left."

He goes to the kitchen and brings one of the bottles he had hidden in the cupboard, behind the pots. He pours two drinks in paper cups.

"I'm in no mood to party, Jason. Not after partying the whole night," she says, and takes one swig from the cup. "Now give me my keys."

He pats his pockets once more and pretends he can't find the keys. Rachel laughs and says that is a cheap trick. He was just driving her car a few minutes ago; there is no way he could have lost the keys between the car and the quilting room. Jason reaches for her and holds both her hands while gently swinging her arms.

"You can give me a goodnight kiss though, won't you?"

She gives him a peck on the cheek.

"Come on, a real kiss, not some fuckin' baby kiss."

"You know you're like a brother to me, Jason," she says trying to free her hands. But his grip is tight.

"I ain't nobody's brother," he says.

"My pops played marbles with Genesis when they were kids," she says, trying in vain to lighten the moment.

"So fuckin' what?" he says. "Doesn't even make us kissin' cousins then?"

He grabs her to himself and holds her tightly. She tries to push him away, but he is too strong. He plants a wet kiss on her lips as she screams: "No, Jason! Let me go!"

She is really fighting back now, kicking him on the shins and elbowing him on his ribcage. He won't let her free, so she sinks her teeth into his hand.

"Holy fuck, that hurt!" he screams.

He slaps her repeatedly on the face, and then throws her roughly on the floor. She is still kicking and screaming as he drags her to a particular spot. He leaps to the drawer of one of the sewing chests and gets a pair of scissors. She tries to escape but he grabs her before she reaches the door, and once more drags her back to the special area—the spot he used to clean incessantly.

"If you don't stop screaming I'll use this," he says, brandishing the scissors.

She curls into a fetal position, whimpering.

"So, we can't kiss, hey?" he says, hovering over her. "We'll fuck then? How do you like that?"

He is on his knees, and he uncurls her, forcing her legs open. He kneels between them. He then rips her Santa Claus costume with the scissors: first the velvet top, then the miniskirt and the knickers. She spits on his face, and follows that with an attempted knee to the groin.

"Holy shit! What you gonna try next?"

More slaps on the face. She gives up. She just lies there as he takes his pants down and crashes on her.

"So you wanna gag, hey?" His tone is no longer menacing. It is gentle.

She does not know what he is talking about. Does not associate it with anything. But yes, she feels nausea; the Old Spice reeks all over him, and she retches.

"You can't tell me you still wanna gag. I cleaned myself for you. Since that day when you told 'em you wanna gag, I cleaned and cleaned so I smell good now. For you."

He spits these last two words out with so much venom that she recoils. He forcefully opens her legs with his knees.

As he does his business on her, she tries to ignore the pain thrust into her and the cold of the linoleum floor. Think of other things, she tells herself. The trick had always worked when she was little. Whenever she was in trouble, she just switched off from the present and thought of the good times. Maybe when her pops was still alive. Maybe when he first brought her Blue and she was freaked out by her. Maybe when he drew the eyes and the nose and the mouth with a pen. By the time she switched on back to the present, the trouble would be gone.

He kicks the leg of the table; frosted slabs come tumbling on the floor from the wobbly gingerbread houses, forcing her to the present. She struggles once more to let her mind wander. She can forget the humiliation that surges into her chest for a while. The humiliation and the anger. But his smell forces her back to the business at hand. The cologne is very unsettling. As if what he is doing to her would have been less horrendous if he had retained his high-school odor. Or at least if there were traces of the old smell disguised with patchouli. It does not matter that she does not know how patchouli smells. Does not know how it looks either. She only knows that it is reputed in folklore as hippy perfume. And Jason is a hippy. As was his father before him. Before he found Jesus. Jesus. Perhaps if she thinks about Jesus he will come and save her. She is no churchgoer. Never been one. Neither is Nana Moira. But Jesus is said to be all-loving and all-forgiving. He does not only save churchgoers.

He is whispering something. No, not Jesus.

"See? It ain't so bad, is it?"

"Fuck you, Jason!" she says, and starts weeping again. She is angry that he has forced her back to the reality she was trying to forget, to what she has been trying to push to that corner of the brain where all bad memories are stored even as it is happening. Do the impossible. Turn present experience into memory.

"You fuck so good when you're mad at me, my Rache. I love you, Rachie. You belong to me, not to

Skye. I am more of a man than Skye. Now you know, hey Rache? Now you know who's the man."

It dawns on her that Jason is replaying her love-making with Skye—a more savage and brutal version of it. He must have seen them.

He jerks into convulsions as he ejaculates into her.

He stands and pulls his pants up. She is a tattered bundle of sobs on the floor. He gently helps her up. The pieces of Santa Claus costume fall off and she is naked.

"You can't go to Nana Moira like this," he says. "What the fuck are we gonna do, Rache?"

"I just wanna pee," she says.

He lets her go to the bathroom while he looks for something to cover her with. He finds a quilt—one of the women's work-in-progress. Maybe Nana Moira's.

"I got something for you, Rache," he says.

But Rachel does not respond. She is no longer there. She is running home with the wind piercing ice-cold needles into her body, making her run even faster. The gravel on the uneven and potholed bitumen road bites into the soles of her feet, but she keeps on running. Dawn paints the horizon red, and semen runs down her thighs. Fortunately no one is up yet at that hour to witness the sight.

"Rache!" Jason's voice echoes in the thin light. "Come back, Rache. Here's your key, I can drive you home. I got a quilt for you! R-a-a-a-a-che!"

Nana Moira never gets to see Rachel's limp body stumbling in. It is a blessing that they live in a kind of a neighborhood where people don't bother locking their doors. She creeps into her room like a wounded animal.

The morning after Christmas, Rachel is still locked in her room. On Christmas day, Nana Moira went to the Center to clean up and found Jason waiting at the door, shivering in the cold. They only talked about Rachel when she wanted to know why she left her car at the Center and how she got home.

"Maybe she was too wasted to drive."

Nana Moira left it at that.

When Rachel was certain that her grandma had left, she went out of her room to the bathroom and took a long shower. She scrubbed her body with an exfoliating sponge over and over again. She didn't care that it was adding to the pain. All she wanted was to remove the filth from her body.

When Nana Moira returned, she had locked herself in her room again. Nana Moira was with Jason and they both knocked at her door, asking her to come out.

"Jason wants to talk to you, Rachel, open the door," said Nana Moira. "Whatever you two quarreled about, it's better to talk than lock yourself in your room like a spoilt brat."

"I've brought you Christmas lunch, Rache," said Jason. "I drove to Athens and got you a nice Christmas lunch from Applebee's. You gonna like it, Rache."

The voice sent Rachel retching, especially the "Rache" part. She would never want anyone to call her that again. She covered her head with a comforter but the voices at her door continued. Until finally they gave up.

That night Nana Moira was too tired to wake up to find out what was happening when she heard Rachel running the shower even though it was after midnight. She wondered why she ran it for such a long time, but fell asleep before she could muster strength to wake up and investigate.

Again this morning Rachel has not left her room, except to take a shower. She has not touched the Applebee's food. She has not eaten anything—second day running. She has decided that's the best way to kill herself: just stop eating. But she will die clean. She sneaks back into the bathroom and takes another shower. And another. After every few minutes, a shower.

She needs to take as many of them as possible because once Nana Moira returns from the Center she won't be able to go for another one. Until after midnight when she is certain that Nana Moira is asleep. So while she is away she scrubs her body incessantly. She does not even spare the wounded vagina. Despite the pain she scrubs it, and she scrubs the wounded sole of her feet. She weeps at the piercing pain but does not stop scrubbing.

After almost a week, Rachel has still not eaten and Nana Moira cannot get through to her. She swallows her pride and says, "I'm gonna get that floozy Schuyler to talk to her."

5

She won't open even for her best friend. Schuyler pounds on the door with her fist, calling her name. Rachel does not respond. Nana Moira paces the floor behind Schuyler. Schuyler has never seen Nana Moira displaying any sign of nervousness before. She has always been as tough as a crowbar and nothing could faze her, until now. Schuyler does not give a rat's behind for her because of all the names Nana Moira has called her in an attempt to break her friendship with Rachel. So she was surprised when she saw Nana Moira's GMC Suburban on her driveway. Though she was waiting for an instructor who was going to teach her how to drive her pick-up van—newly modified with adaptive devices—she did not hesitate to postpone the lesson. She got into Nana Moira's vehicle and they sped to Jensen Township.

"Can you hear me, Rache?" asks Schuyler. There is no response.

Rachel can hear her all right. She is coiled into a fetal position under a comforter, whimpering, with Blue in her arms and a pillow on her face in a futile attempt to shut out the annoying sounds. She retches at "Rache."

"Rachel, please don't be like this," says Schuyler. She would be saying "Don't be an asshole" if Nana Moira were not here. She would be ferreting her out with a slew of cusswords as only a close friend can. But she is a girl from the hills and was raised to respect old age even when it does not respect itself.

"I'm not going anywhere, Rachel," she says. "I'm gonna sit here till you open."

And indeed she pulls a chair and sits right in front of the door. For a while Nana Moira does not know what to do with herself, and Schuyler ignores her. But later Nana Moira decides to go get busy at the Center.

The clock ticks slowly for Schuyler. She should have brought a magazine to read. Occasionally she reminds her friend, "I'm still here, Rachel." She switches on the television. Though she cannot see the screen from where she sits, she can follow from the audio the daytime drivel of lovers caught cheating and being chased down the streets of American cities with cameras.

At the Center Jason is sitting at the table, silently staring at the floor. The quilting women tease him: How come he has not mopped the floor since Christmas Eve? But he does not respond, does not participate in any of their banter either, which is quite unusual. They try to find out if he is not feeling well. He responds curtly that he is fine. As soon as he hears Nana Moira's GMC Suburban park outside he rushes out to meet her.

"How's Rachel? What's she say is her problem?"

"She won't talk to nobody. Not even to Schuyler."

Nana Moira stings Jason with her eyes and demands that he tells her what happened between them. He fidgets. His eyes dart from one place to another, then rest on the concrete paving. Not once do they even try to work their way up to Nana Moira's face.

"Why d'you think it's got to do with me, Nana Moira?"

"'Cause I'm a grown-ass woman, my boy. She was with you on Christmas Eve all by yourself when everybody else was gone. You left with her and Schuyler. She tell me you dropped her at her house and drove away. So, what did you and Rachel get up to?"

Jason realizes that his shifty eyes render him a suspect. He attempts to re-establish eye contact with Nana Moira. But he cannot outdare her, so his eyes seek refuge on the paving again.

"Okay, I'm gonna fess up," he says. "Me and Rachel, we got wasted and high and did stuff we shouldn't done."

"So, you turned my Center into a whorehouse? That doesn't account for the awful bad state she's in right now."

"We quarreled afterwards," says Jason.

It was all about Skye Riley. Now that they had consummated their relationship, he felt entitled to express his objection to her liaison with the coal miner from West Virginia. She, on the other hand, was insisting that she would not cut ties with the man. Jason then brought up an incident that he had witnessed that day Skye graced them with a visit. An incident about which he had told no one until then. He had seen through the window Rachel "doing the dirty" with Skye on Nana Moira's own unfinished quilt. Hoping to black-mail her into breaking up with Skye he threatened to tell Nana Moira about it. That's when she threw a tantrum and dashed out of the Center, running all the way home leaving her car parked where Nana Moira found it later the next morning. Perhaps that's why she does not want to talk to anybody. She is ashamed of what she did with Skye, and then with Jason on that Christmas morning after leading him on.

At that very moment Rachel is telling a different story.

She had to open finally. It was midday already and she wanted to pee so badly. She couldn't hold it any longer. She also wanted to take a shower. It had been hours since she took one and already the filth of Christmas morning was building up on her body, and especially on her vagina, rendering it unlovable. So she got out of bed and tiptoed to the door. She stood there for a while, contemplating the door as if it was something to be feared.

"Schuyler," she whispered. Her voice was hoarse.

"I'm still here, Rache," said Schuyler.

"Please, leave me alone. I just wanna be alone. I'll be fine, promise."

"I'm not going anywhere, Rache."

She opened the door, and Schuyler was shocked how emaciated she had become in these few days. She was covered only in a towel. Her eyes were red and puffy as she glared down at her.

"Don't you fuckin' call me that ever again," she said.

"Call what?"

"My name is Rachel. Rachel. Not anything else but Rachel."

She walked past Schuyler's chair and went straight to the bathroom. She was there for a long time. Schuyler could hear water running as she tried to push the door open. But Rachel had bolted it. Schuyler gave up and sat on the couch. She watched endless daytime talk shows and TV judges passing judgment on petty cases until Rachel, all red as if she had been cooked, walked out of the bathroom. Schuyler reached for her to embrace her but Rachel cringed and gave one long yelp.

"I don't give a damn what you say, I'm taking you to the hospital," said Schuyler.

"I just need to get high on something," said Rachel. "Then I'm gonna feel better."

"Like a reefer or something?'

"Like a reefer or something," Rachel whispered back.

"What the fuck!" Schuyler stood back to give her a long look. It was no secret that her late boyfriend was a stoner and she was the enabler. She knew all the places where one could score weed, but she was not about to indulge this obviously very sick woman with any such stuff. Instead she insisted that she was taking her to the hospital, and if she didn't cooperate she was going to call the sheriff.

"You wouldn't," said Rachel, feebly defiant. "I didn't do any crime."

Schuyler dared Rachel to stop her. She would tell the sheriff that Rachel was on the verge of killing herself and he surely would send a deputy. When Rachel broke down weeping, Schuyler gently led her to the couch.

It is here that she is telling her story, drastically different from the version Jason is telling Nana Moira. It comes in jerks and sobs. For almost a week she has refrained from talking about this. She has even tried to avoid thinking about it. Just as she tried to avoid thinking about it even as it was happening. But the nightmares have continued to intrude, replaying the rape in grotesque dramas. In some of them she attempts to rape Jason. He is screaming and running away from her all over the quilt room, and then poof!—he just disappears. In another one that recurs only when she is not sleeping with Blue, it is just the boots that are chasing her. Jason's boots, she surmises, though she has never paid enough attention to the man's boots to be able to identify them. At first she doesn't understand why she is able to see the fine details of the hiking boots, including the grain on the leather and thick black soles, even though she is running away from them. Then she realizes that she can also see herself running away naked, as if she is also her own spectator. She wakes up screaming, switches on the bedside lamp and looks for Blue. She finds Blue lying on the floor, having been pushed out of the bed by her kicks and swings as she battled the demons of her nightmares.

Rachel does not tell Schuyler about the nightmares. Just what happened that Christmas morning. The parts that she can force herself to remember.

"And you did nothing about this? You didn't call the cops?"

Rachel tells her she does not want to involve the police because people will talk.

"Who the fuck cares what people say?" asks Schuyler. "You've been raped, Rachel. You don't just sit there and let this guy get away with it."

She should have called the sheriff immediately, says Schuyler. She shouldn't have taken a bath until seen by a doctor. After a week she has washed away all the evidence.

"I am not going to call the police, Schuyler," she says emphatically and deliberately.

"Oh, yes, you will," says Schuyler with as much deliberation. "If you don't I will."

"It was my fault," cries Rachel. "I led him on. People are going to talk. I don't wanna have anything to do with this anymore. Please Schuyler, leave the law out of this."

Schuyler finds a telephone directory and phones the sheriff's office in Athens. If it is something that happened almost a week ago there is no urgency about it, the receptionist says, especially with a number of emergencies today and the staff shortage due to budget cuts. They always make it a point to tell the callers that, hoping they will put pressure on the politicians. The receptionist assures Schuyler that she will send a deputy later in the afternoon.

Schuyler cajoles Rachel to drink some milk. She retches and runs to the bathroom. When she returns, Schuyler tries again, just a small sip at a time. Then she leads her to the bedroom and helps her put on her clothes. It can't be pants or anything tight. It has to be a very loose dress, and Rachel has none of those. So, Schuyler goes to raid Nana Moira's wardrobe and returns with a floral dress that droops on Rachel's shoulders. She looks ridiculous but doesn't care. She will have to do without any underwear.

Nana Moira returns later that afternoon and is shocked at how her granddaughter looks. Clearly she is sick and needs medical attention, but she decides not to create any drama about it lest she retreats to her room again, never to emerge alive.

"Why are you in my dress?" she asks.

This question annoys Schuyler so much that she hisses straight at Nana Moira's face: "Is that all you care about—your stupid dress?"

"Yeah, 'cause she looks like a scarecrow in it," she says. "Her own clothes are more nicer than an old woman's gingham."

Then she breaks into her cackling laughter. But no one joins her. Her laughter is stopped by the arrival of a deputy. She demands to know why the law is at her house and who called without consulting her. Schuyler curtly tells her to shut up because Rachel was raped and she doesn't even know about it even though they live in the same house. The deputy suggests that he talks privately with Rachel in the car. Schuyler fears that Rachel will renege and not press charges. She insists that she has to be there because Rachel is so sick that she needs her assistance. The two women and the deputy repair to his car.

Nana Moira will not be bullied by Schuyler, not in her own house, and not about her own granddaughter. She shuffles with her cane to the car and taps the window with it. The deputy opens.

"Who raped who?" she asks.

"I don't know, I'm still taking the statement."

"Jason raped Rachel," says Schuyler.

Rachel retches. Schuyler is quick enough to open the door and Rachel spews the milk on the driveway.

"You gonna send Genesis's boy to jail?" asks Nana Moira, hovering over Rachel's head as it hangs out of the car. She continues to retch without anything coming out anymore. "What did he do to you that you didn't do with nobody else?"

"No, I don't wanna make a statement," cries Rachel. "I just wanna go to my room."

There is no stopping Nana Moira once she gets started.

"She knows what she done with Skye. On my unfinished quilt too. I'll never touch that quilt again."

Schuyler helps the rest of Rachel's limp body into the car and the deputy drives away with the two women. He says the priority is to take Rachel to O'Bleness Hospital for urgent care. They can see about laying the rape charge later.

As the car drives away Nana Moira yells after it: "You have ended up such a hussy, Rachel."

New Year's Day. Jason is the only one at the Center. He has come to tend to the compost. He's been postponing this for some time and fears that if he neglects it any further the system will not survive the winter. He needs to keep it warm so that it stays microbially active.

But it is more than just the compost that has kept him skulking in this neighborhood. He has to be here on the off chance that he spots Rachel. He wants to settle things with her, to explain that he loves her too much to mean her any harm. He can just drive to her house, but Nana Moira has advised him to stay away because Rachel gets hysterical at the mere mention of his name. The Center is the closest he can get to Rachel.

The building is locked because Nana Moira and the quilting women will not be working today. But Jason has no need for anything inside. He has brought with him everything he needs. The compost is only about one cubic yard; he has enough corrugated cardboard for insulation. He lines the bin with a few layers and adds more cardboard between the outer wall of the bin and the insulation layer. On top of the bin he spreads a bedding of old clothes that have been donated for the poor but didn't have any takers. The women usually use some of these as batting for their quilts. He remembers that there is something he needs in the building after all—the old scraps from the Christmas dinner. Nana Moira kept them in a bucket next to the stove. It is the fresh waste he needs to keep the system chugging for a month or two before he adds more waste.

He walks to the front and contemplates the door. He tries it. It is indeed locked. He'll have to wait until Nana Moira decides to open the Center for business again.

"Jason de Klerk?"

He turns around and faces two deputies, a male and a female. He had not noticed their car parked outside the gate. They read him his Miranda rights and handcuff him.

Nana Moira does not hear of Jason's arrest until two days later when Genesis comes bumbling into the Center, demanding to talk with her privately. It is the first day at work after the New Year festivities and only two other members of the Quilting Circle have showed up. They noticed at once that Nana Moira was not quite her boisterous self. Instead of being up and about she just sat on the chair, brooding. One of the women offered to brew some coffee for her and she is sipping it as she hobbles out to the porch with Genesis.

"My boy has landed in the slammer for something he didn't do," says Genesis. "And you didn't tell me nothing about it."

"I didn't know about it," says Nana Moira.

"They arrested him right here at the Center and you tell me you didn't know?"

Nana Moira tells him that it is only the first day the Center has opened since Christmas, so if Jason was ever here before today she knows nothing about that. All she knows is that she was with Rachel and Schuyler when the law arrived in the form of a deputy from the sheriff's office and left with the two "girls" after accusing Jason of raping Rachel. She has not seen Rachel since, and is worried out of her mind. It would not be that big a deal because sometimes she does visit with that floozy Schuyler for a couple of days, but she always says where she is at. She's been calling her cell phone and no one answers. She can't bring herself to call Schuyler's house after the insulting way she behaved towards her that day.

"Revelation can't rape nobody," says Genesis.

"Sweet grief, what kind of god-awful name is that?" says Nana Moira. "Just call the boy Jason and get it over with."

"It don't matter about the name, Nana Moira. My boy is in the pen."

Genesis sits on one of the car seats, his head resting in his hands. Nana Moira puts her cane and the mug of coffee on the floor and sits next to him. They are lost in contemplation for a while.

"I've taught the boy many things about life, but raping women is not one of them," Genesis finally says.

After Genesis leaves Nana Moira reaches for her bookkeeping records and tries to tally figures on some vouchers. But her mind wanders to Rachel wherever she might be. And to Jason in a jail cell. Things wouldn't have come to this if only Rachel had confided in her. She would have advised her differently. Genesis is like family. Stuff like this should be handled within the family, without bringing the law into it. Whatever happened between them was a misunderstanding, a result of Christmas inebriation. She can no longer focus on the ledgers and journals. She will not be able to focus on anything until she finds Rachel and gives her a long hug and then talks some sense into her. She will swallow her pride and drive to Schuyler's and return with her granddaughter. She regrets why she involved Schuyler in the first place. She should have handled things herself right from the beginning.

"We gonna lock up early today, it being our first day and all," she tells the two women. They are not putting in much work anyway.

Nana Moira is a bit exercised when she gets home and finds a beat up pick-up truck parked on her spot. She parks right behind it and waddles to the trailer, intent on telling off whoever has the gumption to park on her space. She stands at the door and emits a loud sigh of relief: there is Rachel and Schuyler sitting on the couch and giggling like school girls.

"Thank you Sweet Jesus, you are back!"

"Nana Moira!" Rachel jumps up, rushes to her grandma and gives her a big hug.

Nana Moira is amazed to see the change in Rachel. She is still emaciated but color has returned to her cheeks and her eyes have some brightness in them. They are less hollow than they were when she left three days ago. Obviously she has been eating some.

There is another thing too that is strange. The room. Not only has the furniture been rearranged, but the couch is completely different. It is now a sofa in bright red faux leather. Rachel flings herself on the sofa and she and Schuyler huddle together drinking diet soda.

"How do you like it, Nana Moira?"

"You changed everything without telling me."

"It's my house, Nana Moira. I do what I like with it."

Technically she is correct. Nana Moira only came to live with Rachel and her parents when her truck farm was foreclosed. Rachel is known to occasionally throw that at Nana Moira's face whenever they have a disagreement on how things should be done in the house.

Rachel giggles some more and gestures to her grandma to join them on the three-seater. Nana Moira hesitates, but before she moves to take the seat, Schuyler says, "Come on, Nana Moira, don't be such a downer."

She shouldn't have spoken. Nana Moira gives her the evil eye, and walks to her bedroom. She remains there until Rachel comes to ask for the keys of her GMC Suburban to move it out of the way of Schuyler's pick-up truck.

"You should see it, Nana Moira," says Rachel. "It's so cool."

"It's all beat up and ugly," says Nana Moira, handing her the keys and turning her back to her. Rachel doesn't seem to notice her gesture; she is bubbling all over the place.

"You should see it inside," she says. "Everything is hand-controlled: the breaking, steering, and acceleration systems."

"Never seen a steering that's foot-controlled anyways."

"She was lucky the Fed did it for her. It costs a fortune to adapt a car for the disabled, you know?"

"You gonna be crippled like her too if you keep that kinda company."

Rachel ignores the remark and goes to remove the car. Then she goes to her bedroom. She retrieves Blue from the floor and sits on the bed caressing her. Soon Nana Moira taps at her door with her cane. Without waiting for her response she enters and sits on the bed next to her. She holds her in her arms.

"I'm glad to see you're so happy," she says.

"I'm done with not being happy," says Rachel.

Even though her grandma treats Schuyler so rudely, she says, it helped staying with her for a couple of days. She could have stayed longer but it is too crowded and chaotic there. Schuyler's mom, dad, and three brothers just hang around the house, drinking and yelling at one another and strewing stuff all over the floor. None of them is working and they all depend on SNAP, soup kitchens, and food pantries for their survival. It didn't help that Rachel had mood swings most of the time. She would be happy and smiling one time, in tears the next. She slept with Schuyler in her bedroom, and because she didn't have Blue with her, she sometimes woke up screaming from the nightmares. And when that happened the whole household woke up. Although Schuyler was patient and understanding, her folks couldn't cope with her. They were dismissive of her experience and didn't think it was any big deal.

She overheard the brothers laughing about it. "I can't imagine Jason doing it right with his foolish hippy dick," said one brother. "Hippies got dicks too?" asked another brother. The third one would not be outdone. "Floppy hippy prick," he said, and they all broke out laughing. They didn't even seem embarrassed when they saw her standing there. As far as they were concerned it was not about her, but about Jason. They didn't reckon she would feel that her rape was being reduced to a joke.

She knew it was time to leave.

She missed her Nana Moira. And she missed her home. But she couldn't face it the way it was. She wanted a change in the house that would suit the change that has come over her. She took advantage of Schuyler's pick-up and transported the old couch to Goodwill in Athens, and bought another used one there. With Schuyler's help, though limited by her mobility problems, she rearranged the furniture. As soon as she had accomplished that, she was overwhelmed by effervescent joy that continues till now.

"That couch was still good, Rachel. You just wanna spend money for nothing."

Rachel laughs and says Nana Moira is famous for her miserly ways. She doesn't like to spend money for anything. Even the women at the Center always tease her that she holds on to the nickel until Thomas Jefferson squeals.

Nana Moira wants Rachel's happiness to last. She observes that she hasn't touched her guitar for a long time. Maybe she should start playing and busking and everything will be normal again.

"I'm never going to be playing again, Nana Moira. Everybody knows that I suck. I'm not going to be anything ever."

"You can go to Hocking. Learn the thing you wanted to learn and be somebody like you always wanted to be. If it's not music it can be something else."

"I don't wanna be anything. I don't deserve to be anything."

Then she breaks out laughing. She looks so happy Nana Moira thinks it is unnatural. Her Rachel has always been the brooding type. But now she is so wide-eyed and carefree.

"I fear for you, you know that, my baby?" says Nana Moira.

"Why would you be scared for me, Nana Moira? We gonna be fine."

"We not gonna be fine, Rachel. As long as Genesis's boy is in the pokey we not gonna be fine. He's like family to us."

Rachel continues to be bubbly.

"Well, I'll be fine regardless."

"This'll haunt us for ever. You must withdraw that case."

"No," says Rachel firmly, and then stands up to glare at her grandma.

"What if he gets right? You won't forgive him?"

"If you're going to harp on that, I'll leave again."

Nana Moira loses her patience with her and stamps her feet.

"You don't wanna do nothing I tell you, Rachel. I'm your grandma and I love you."

Rachel laughs and sits on the bed next to Nana Moira and embraces her.

"Okay, Nana Moira, I'll go to the sheriff to withdraw the case. I'll tell them I was mistaken, it didn't happen the way I said it did. Anyways, I've come to realize it was my fault. Whatever happened was my fault."

Nana Moira hugs her back. They are locked in each other's arms for a long time. She then leaves after kissing her granddaughter on the cheek.

She is at the stove frying pork which she is going to pile on tortilla chips with cheddar—a treat for Rachel—when she hears a piercing scream from Rachel's bedroom. She rushes in and finds Rachel tearing into things like a raging bull. Her whole bedding is on the floor and she is screaming as she rips posters of country singers from the wall. As Nana Moira appeals to her to calm down, she grabs the lamp from the nightstand and smashes it on the floor. She reaches for Blue on the floor and tries to tear her apart, but Blue is too strong. She flings her across the room. Nana Moira reaches for Rachel and tries to restrain her. Rachel doesn't resist. Nana Moira staggers with her to the bed and they sit. She melts in her grandma's arms. She is gasping and sobbing as her grandma rocks her as she used to when she was a baby.

"It's gonna be all right, baby; it's gonna be fine," Nana Moira keeps repeating.

She parks her car at the City Parking Garage and contemplates the meter. She is not sure how many quarters she should insert because she has no idea how long her business will be. She inserts four hours' worth of quarters and walks out of the garage, along Washington Street. She then crosses Court Street and walks into the Athens County Court House. She places her handbag on the conveyer belt and walks through the security checkpoint. She takes the elevator to the third floor.

Schuyler is already waiting on a bench near the door of Judge Alexander Stonebrook's court. They exchange greetings and huddle together quietly, watching people as they go in and out of the offices and courtrooms that open to the foyer. Occasionally the elevator opens and people trickle out and take the other benches. They all look serious, which is understandable since most of them are parties to some litigation or witnesses or relatives of accused persons. They all wait quietly.

"There is a lot of waiting here," Schuyler whispers to Rachel. "You'll get used to it."

She is talking from experience. She spent days, even weeks, waiting on these benches when she was on trial for stealing the ashes of her boyfriend. Rachel also knows what she is talking about. She has waited on two occasions before. But she does not respond; she is trying to deal with her dread.

A prisoner in an orange jumpsuit and manacles on his hands and feet walks out of the elevator, followed by a police officer. His face brightens when he recognizes two women sitting on the opposite bench. They smile back at him. The prisoner is led to a bench next to the door of another judge's court. The two women are allowed to join him there.

A tall, lean man in a dirty, fawn, striped suit enters and perches himself on the far end of Rachel's bench without as much as giving anyone a glance. He is so comfortable and sure of himself that everyone can see that these are his haunts. He takes out a book from his pocket and reads. From time to time an attorney comes looking for his client and chit-chats with the man before dashing into the courtroom or the elevator.

"He's a journalist from the *Athens News*," whispers Schuyler.

This piece of information unsettles Rachel.

"He's going to write about this case? It's going to be in the newspaper?"

"If he thinks it's interesting enough."

"I don't want to be in the newspaper. People are going to talk."

"They're going to talk anyways. No big deal."

The prisoner is quite a chatterbox. The two women are laughing at some yarn he is narrating animatedly despite the shackles. You could have sworn they are chilling in their own living room without any care in the world. None of them seem to be apprehensive of the proceedings that will be taking place involving them today. The officer guarding the man sits on a nearby bench and occasionally laughs along with the prisoner and the women.

Rachel looks at them enviously. If only she could be as relaxed. This is the third occasion she has had to come to this court, and every time she has sat here, she has endured stomach cramps and dizziness and nausea and sweaty palms and a fast heartbeat.

It was worse on the first occasion. She was by herself because Schuyler had a job interview. She whiled away time by observing people getting out of the elevator and imagining what they could be here for. She wondered how some of them could be so cheery in a gloomy, wood-paneled place like this. Some of them were workers—young law graduates clerking for some judge, secretaries, and attorneys. She could never imagine herself being happy working here.

Her anxiety worsened when Genesis walked out of the elevator with a beautiful middle-aged woman. She had a sophisticated and confident look. She was so impeccably dressed and groomed that Rachel concluded she was not from Athens. She was right. The woman was Kayla Trenta from Columbus, regarded as the foremost sexual-offenses lawyer in the state. She prides herself for putting together the best courtroom defense and for winning some of the toughest cases in the various county courts throughout Ohio. She is well-beloved by alleged felons because the first thing she says on the initial consultation is that she never passes any moral judgment as to the circumstances of the case and therefore the client should talk freely. She is also in great demand and therefore very expensive.

Kayla Trenta walked into the courtroom and Genesis sat on one of the benches. Although he was almost opposite Rachel, he didn't give her as much as a glance. She felt very bad for putting Genesis through all this pain. He had always been such a nice man. And very generous too. Often he donated the extra produce from his garden to the Center. And now he has to sit here for hours on end all because of her. She felt pangs of guilt. She wanted to go to him, kneel before him, apologize, and tell him that she was sorry that she called the sheriff in the first place. It was all Schuyler's fault. Okay, it was her fault too because she went along with that. She wanted to tell him that she had wanted to withdraw the case; she had been determined to do so after promising Nana Moira. But again Schuyler had intervened. She stubbornly had driven to the sheriff's office regardless. Schuyler had chased her in her pick-up truck. As she breathlessly told the deputy at the desk that she wanted to withdraw the case, Schuyler had hobbled in and had told the deputy that Rachel was out of her mind; what she went through had made her unstable. She would regret later if she withdrew the case. The deputy had sided with Schuyler and tried to persuade her to proceed with the case. In any event, the deputy had added, the matter was with the prose-cuting authorities and Rachel did not have the power to withdraw it if they thought the accused had a case to answer. It was no longer Rachel's case; it was the State of Ohio versus Jason de Klerk.

She wanted to confess all this to Genesis, like a pen-itent hoping for absolution. She stole a glance at him; his pained expression disabused her at once of any notion of seeking release from him. So, she just sat there and waited and fought the urge to take another glance at him.

The elevator opened and out walked two police officers with Jason in orange coveralls and manacles on hands and feet. A brief moment of panic as their eyes locked. She buried her head in her hands between the knees, trying very hard to stop the urge to take to her heels. But not before she noticed that Jason had gained a lot of weight in the three months since the incident. It couldn't just be the oversized coveralls. His face was puffy.

Jason was led into the courtroom and Genesis followed. As no one bothered to tell Rachel what was happening, she stood up and looked through the glass door. There was no one else in the court except Jason sitting by himself on a bench and Genesis sitting behind him. The police officers were sitting a distance away. Rachel was pleased that they were at least giving father and son the opportunity to talk.

She went back to sit on the bench.

No one informed her that at that very moment Judge Alexander Stonebrook was listening to heated arguments from Kayla Trenta and the prosecutor, Dylan Holton, in a closed hearing. Trenta had submitted a motion that the defense be allowed to introduce evidence about Rachel's previous sex life. She also wanted to be allowed to question Rachel and other witnesses individually before the trial to determine whether the sheriff's office had placed undue influence on Rachel to proceed with the case when she wanted to withdraw it. Trenta submitted that the alleged victim wanted to withdraw the case because she knew that the count of rape against her client—a first-degree felony that could land a poor, innocent man in jail for life—was false. The prosecutor, on the other hand, was arguing that Ohio's rape shield laws prohibited an accused rapist from presenting evidence about the alleged victim's previous sex life unless it had direct bearing on the alleged rape. Trenta argued that the evidence that the defense would present about sexual relations between Rachel and one Skye Riley, a coal miner from West Virginia, had direct bearing. She did not elaborate, but Holton knew how wily Trenta was and how easily and logically she could connect the dots on unrelated incidents and convince the jury that one was a result of the other.

As these arguments were going on in the judge's chambers Rachel sat there waiting. She pulled out her cell phone from her handbag, hoping to play a game or text Schuyler, but the darn thing was dead. She had forgotten to charge the battery that morning. Perhaps she should have brought a book, she thought, though she was not much of a book reader. Perhaps a magazine. Or a newspaper. All boring stuff, but it would have helped to while away the time. If only she had her guitar. That would have done it. On second thoughts, no. It would not have done it. She didn't ever want to touch that guitar again. Or any guitar. She hated everything about it. About music. About her whiny voice which she didn't even know was whiny until Skye Riley told her so. Skye Riley. She had not thought of him all this time. Three months since the thing happened and she had not thought of Skye Riley once.

The sound of shackles interrupted this trend of thought. It was Jason being led out of the courtroom to the elevator. He made a point of looking at Rachel and smile. She quickly looked away. Genesis soon followed and walked straight to the elevator without even a glance at her. After some time Dylan Holton came out and told her she could go home. Lawyers were arguing of things she shouldn't bother herself about. She wondered why she was required to be here in the first place if this was lawyers' business and not hers.

That was the first occasion she had waited here for hours and left livid. The second occasion was a week later. She went straight to her bench like a homing pigeon. This time Schuyler was with her, so things were slightly better. She talked incessantly, commenting on the fellow waiters or hazarding a guess as to the crimes of manacled prisoners in orange coveralls. At one time an officer shushed her, but after only thirty minutes or so, she was back with her running commentary.

The panic hit Rachel again when they brought Jason in, and then there was the parade of the usual characters: Genesis in his dungarees and plaid shirt and muddy boots, Kayla Trenta looking like she walked out of a fashion magazine, and Dylan Holton traipsing about as if the floor would crack. They walked into the courtroom leaving her out there like before.

Holton and Trenta went into Judge Stonebrook's chambers while Jason, Genesis, and the police officers remained in the courtroom.

This time Rachel's wait was not that long. The judge was only a few minutes with counsel, informing them that he was denying Trenta's pre-trial motions. There would be no individual voir dire questioning of Rachel and any other witness on whether the Sheriff's office had an undue influence when Rachel wanted to withdraw the case. Also, the shield law would be observed and the defense was barred from using any evidence of the alleged victim's sexual history. The prosecutor told Rachel and Schuyler that they could go home. Once more Rachel wondered why she had been asked to be there in the first place.

This third occasion she hopes things will be different; the case will proceed and she will be done with waiting here with all the hostile and curious eyes stinging her. The stomach cramps and dizziness have returned and she wishes she were at home sleeping on her bed, which is what she does most of the time these days. Since she returned from her brief exile at Schuyler's home, she spends most of the days in her room with only Blue for company. Until Schuyler comes every other day or so for a visit. Rarely does she visit Schuyler because she finds her brothers annoying.

The chatterbox prisoner in orange coveralls is still entertaining his guests. Rachel reckons the older woman is his mother and the younger one, his sister. Or perhaps his wife? He looks rather young to have a wife. She wonders what he has been charged with and why he doesn't seem to be concerned. Why his relatives seem to be unconcerned too. Perhaps he is such a habitual criminal that these environs have become home to him and his family.

Her speculations are interrupted by Genesis who walks out of the elevator. This time he is with his wife. They enter the courtroom. So does the *Athens News* journalist and a few other people who are obviously spectators. Schuyler indicates to Rachel that they must also go in. They take a seat on the back row where Rachel hopes they will not be conspicuous.

She has never been inside a court before and her eyes explore the room, from the Great Seal of the State of Ohio at the center of the wall she is facing, with the American flag on the left and the state flag on the right, to the stained-glass windows on the left and the right of the judge's bench. One window portrays Lady Justice holding her golden scales and the other a woman taking an oath on the Bible. On the walls there are black-and-white photographs of Athens County Bar Association members for various years.

Soon Jason and his lawyer enter. One can easily mistake him for a lawyer himself, in a black suit, a white shirt, a black tie, and black shoes. He is only betrayed by the manacles on his hands and feet. He walks with difficulty, every step accompanied by the clink of chains. He is clean-shaven both on the face and the head. Kayla Trenta is glamorous in a black pantsuit, a white blouse and strings of pearls on her neck. Schuyler whispers to Rachel that the color coordination of lawyer and client is a deliberate attempt to sway the jury. She does not provide the answer when Rachel asks how this is supposed to sway the jury and why there is no jury in the jury box to be swayed anyway.

People all rise when Judge Alexander Stonebrook enters and only sit when he has taken his seat at the bench. He announces that the accused, Jason de Klerk, also known as Revelation de Klerk, was scheduled to take a plea bargain today, but he was informed at the last minute this morning that the deal was off. A few days ago the attorney for the accused and the prosecutor had informed the judge that they had worked out a deal and that Jason was prepared to take a plea and probably be sentenced today. One party is accusing the other of reneging on the terms of the plea, although he does not say which party that is. It would seem there is new evidence that makes it impossible for one party to proceed with the previous terms.

All this is a mystery to Rachel. She had not even known that there were any negotiations going on for a plea bargain, and does not understand what that would have entailed. She is puzzled as to the nature of the new evidence that has been discovered. Is it in Jason's favor or in hers? Well, not quite in hers since she is just a bystander in this matter. Is it in favor of the state's case? She has learned to accept that she is the last person that counts in this trial.

"We've been working very hard to get ready for this case," says the judge. "It will have to proceed to trial. Because of scheduling conflicts, this trial can't start for three months at the very least. The trial can't proceed even presuming we can get a jury this month."

Dylan Holton addresses the court.

"I just want to declare in the open court that the state is withdrawing all plea offers," he says.

"That is understood, Mr. Holton," the judge responds. "It is what I have been saying."

"I just want it to be on record, Your Honor."

There is not much that the women can say to each other as Rachel drives Schuyler to Rome Township. She is totally drained and annoyed with herself for allowing Schuyler to bully her into pursuing this case. She should have listened to Nana Moira instead. Now she is going to carry this weight for another three months. She had hoped that today was the last day she would ever have to deal with this matter. She had been convinced that from today everything would be behind her and she would start on a new page.

Another three months of torture and nightmares.

Nana Moira and Rachel are relaxing on the couch, watching the auditions of *American Idol* on television. Rachel is laughing at the antics of aspirant competitors so much that her belly is sore. Nana Moira occasionally cackles but generally thinks it is cruel to put these people through all this ridicule. Instead she is intently looking at Rachel who is laughing so much Nana Moira can see the cheesed puffed cornmeal in her mouth.

"Something is growing in you, Rachel," says Nana Moira out of the blue.

"Whatever you mean, Nana Moira, that's ridiculous."

"I'm a grown-ass woman, Rachel, and I see it all over you. Somebody knocked you up; unless you think am friggin' stupid."

For three months she missed her period. She ignored that. Then she began to throw up. She ignored that too. After all, she had been throwing up a lot from the day she was raped. Any sort of anxiety made her throw up. Then she began to crave Cheetos. The Xxtra Flamin' Hot Crunchy type. Something she never cared about before. She has hated hot spices all her life. But here she was crunching them like nobody's business. Schuyler told her she was pregnant. She said Schuyler was talking crap.

And here is Nana Moira also talking the same crap.

6

There is nothing there. Dead. Whatever was implanted in her womb is dead. It's been dead for months. Now it's just lying there, in her belly, dead. One day the dead weight will just ooze out when she pees and that will be the end of the story. She will forget it ever happened. Ooze out with her period even. Yes, the period will return with all its inconveniences and cramps, and she will be normal again. Until then, she will carry on with her life as if nothing has happened.

She carries the dead weight with her everywhere she goes, though she does not give it a second thought. Until either Nana Moira or Schuyler, the only two people who know about it, bring it up. She hates them when they do.

The old enemies—it is strange how they were on the same side when she discovered she was pregnant. They both wanted her to have an abortion.

The first time Schuyler brought the matter up was three months ago. They were at their haunt, the Skull and Bones Bistro, which is not really a bistro but a bar that's painted black and white inside and serves regular pub grub rather than the French home-style cooking that one expects at an establishment that labels itself a bistro. When Schuyler's stoner-biker boyfriend was still alive, this used to be their trysting place.

Rachel was still in her first trimester when Schuyler raised the matter. Perhaps towards the end of it. One can only guess because she had not gone to a doctor nor taken a pregnancy test of any kind. But both Nana Moira and Schuyler were certain of it just by looking at her, and by observing all the funny things she had developed, like morning sickness and irrational cravings. She, of course, fluctuated between denial and resignation.

"Keeping the baby is like continuing the rape," said Schuyler. "It's going to remind you of it all the time."

This clicked with Rachel. Also, the baby would chain her to Jason for the rest of her life. It made sense to get rid of it. Provided there was a baby. Provided it was Jason's. She took a swig from a beer mug and put it back on the counter.

"What if it's not Jason's? What if it's Skye's?"

"You know that's wishful thinking, dude," said Schuyler, careful not to call her Rache because for some reason that aggravates Rachel. "You told me he used a condom."

"Since when is it hundred percent?"

"Plus you had periods for . . . two months, maybe? . . . after Skye."

She hated Schuyler for knowing so much about her, including her menstrual cycles. She took another gulp. Schuyler did likewise.

"You don't have to carry a product of rape, Rachel."

She understood that too. The first thing that came to her mind when Nana Moira and Schuyler voiced their suspicion that she was pregnant was *oh my gosh, now Jason owns me lock, stock, and barrel!* So, Schuyler was preaching to the choir. But why did she continue to argue against it?

"It will be like being raped over and over again every time you see that kid."

"I don't need convincing," she said as they were leaving the Skull with all those tatted up and leather-jacketed bikers piercing them with their eyes. None had the guts to hit on them because at that time of the morning they had not accumulated enough pot-valiancy. Despite hobbling on a crutch, Schuyler still turned heads, as of course did the willowy Rachel.

They drove away in their separate cars.

Rachel was on Route 50 to Jensen Township when her cell phone buzzed. It was Nana Moira. She wanted to discuss something important with her and was demanding she meet her at the Center. The mere mention of the Center brought palpitations in Rachel. She yelled into the phone that she would not go to the Center for anything. Nana Moira knew that, Rachel added, and yet she wanted to mess with her head.

"If Methuselah won't come to the mountain, then the mountain will come to her."

Rachel couldn't help chuckling. "Something does not sound right somewhere there."

"Of course something's not right when you think you're the mountain and I must leave my work and come to you."

"You're the one who wants to talk." She hung up on her.

Nana Moira did come to the mountain, bringing with her baked goodies. She set them on the coffee table and invited Rachel for a snack while they talked. The same talk Schuyler had with Rachel only an hour or so before. She would have sworn there had been some collusion between the two if they were not such enemies. Rachel was surprised because she had thought her grandma was a pro-lifer. Not that the topic ever arose; she just assumed that everyone of her generation would cringe at the very mention of abortion.

"Motherhood is awful sacred, but only when the young-un is legitimate," said Nana Moira.

As with Schuyler, Rachel did not need any convincing. She told her grandma that it was something she had been considering in any case. She didn't want her to think she was going to do it because of her. Or because of Schuyler. She had been feeling like the puppet of these two women lately, each one pulling the strings in an opposite direction. She would like to assert the fact that she did have a mind of her own.

The next morning she drove to the Planned Parenthood office on East State Street. She was glad that Schuyler had a physio and after that another job interview, otherwise she would have insisted on coming with her. She was determined to see this through herself on her own terms.

She was worried about the money but the receptionist assured her a person of her low income qualified for free services. She didn't have an appointment. Fortunately she didn't have long to wait because the health center was not very busy that morning. After dipping strips in her pee, a chirpy nurse told her she was indeed pregnant—as if she had not known that. And then another clinician dated her pregnancy from the ultrasound; she was about to begin the second trimester.

Rachel told the clinician she wanted an abortion.

"We don't provide abortion services here," said the clinician, "but we'll help you still. We'll give you a referral list of health providers in Athens who offer such services."

She then referred her to a counselor, a kindly middle-aged woman who did more listening than talking. She laid out various options for her, while emphasizing that the choice was solely hers. It was important to learn all the facts about abortion though, to help her make an informed decision. It was also important for her to learn more about parenting and also about adoption in case she decided against abortion.

"I don't want anything to do with that," shrieked Rachel as if the counselor was suggesting she should not go through with the abortion. "This baby is my enemy!"

When she heard that Rachel was raped, she immediately took it for granted that she would automatically want an abortion, and there was no longer any discussion about other options. Instead she explored with her how the procedure could be facilitated with the least inconvenience to her. First, it needed to be done soon, before it was too late. The counselor said the law allowed her to use Medicaid for her abortion, which would otherwise have been illegal had she not been raped.

Rachel felt bouncy when she left the building. It was as though a heavy weight had been lifted from her shoulders. As soon as the mandatory waiting period of twenty-hours was over, she would go to one of the health providers on the list and get rid of the enemy within. The next day would be the day.

It was not the day. Instead she drove to the city, parked her car at the city parking garage, and went from one Court Street bar to the next. In some establishments she was one of only two or three people in the bar, it being weekday and daytime, the regular patrons were either in class at the university or at work. She drank a lot of beer. When she was drunk she texted Schuyler to join her, even though she had sworn to stay away from her because she knew she would be bugging her about the abortion and the dangers of drinking while pregnant and such nonsense. Schuyler could not come. It was late in the evening when Rachel staggered to her car in the city garage. She was too inebriated to drive, so she just slept in the car until the cold woke her at dawn.

The following day was not the day either. She repeated the pattern. But she crowned it with hooking up with a desperate student in the back seat of her car. If beer didn't kill the enemy within, then his dick would. The following morning, she was remorseful and felt filthy. She scrubbed her body to remove the memory.

That was three months ago. Today she would have been six months pregnant. Well, technically she *is* six months pregnant. But the baby died long time ago. Just by itself. Maybe it never lived in the first place. It is just dead weight in her belly. Dead weight. Dead weight.

Dylan Holton tells her she is lucky her case is proceeding after only six months. Normally cases are not on the roll for up to nine months. But, to Rachel, the six months was like a lifetime of torture—what with the dead weight in her belly and the load of impending doom on her shoulders and the woozy state she finds herself in almost every morning and the shame of a random hook-up and the embarrassment of her financial crisis. She has had no income since she stopped busking. She has to ask for gas money from Nana Moira. And for sanitary-pad money. She continues to buy them every month at the time she estimates she would be having her period. She was never one for tampons. She buys pads because she knows that as soon as the dead weight decides to vacate her body, rivers of blood will flow. And she'd better be ready.

Nana Moira also feeds her drinking habit, though she is not aware that's what she does with the money she gives her. She cannot deny her granddaughter a few dollars because Rachel used to share her money liberally when she still had some. However, Nana Moira's meager contribution cannot quench her thirst. Occasionally she gets wasted and stoned, paid for by a random hook-up. These men will poke the dead weight out of her body. They will hasten its departure, and she will be normal again.

Rachel is highly hungover as she sits at the bench near the door of Judge Stonebrook's court. She tries very hard to ignore the ache that wants to split her head into two. She closes her eyes and takes a drink from a water bottle. If only Schuyler were here. But she knows she won't be. She too has her own things to attend to. She said so last night when they were at the Skull.

Last night. She does not want to think about last night. She was raped by Jason. It was only a flashback but it was as real as if he was raping her again. It was after they had been joking about the case that would resume the next day and Schuyler was berating her for her cowardice in not going through with the abortion. She obviously wanted to be tethered to Jason for the rest of her life, Schuyler said.

It began with the smell. A whiff of Old Spice from one of the brawny guys who rubbed against her when he was passing. The scent overwhelmed her and she couldn't breathe. And then the rape happened. Right there at the bar counter, surrounded by all those bikers and their tatted-out biker-bitches—as the ladies call themselves. It was a replay of her experience at the Center in every aspect. Even details she thought she had forgotten. She screamed for help. She was rolling on the floor at the feet of the bikers, screaming as if in pain. Schuyler and a biker-bitch helped her to her feet and tried to calm her down.

"What's the matter, hon?" asked the biker-bitch.

"Nothing," said Rachel, trembling. "Just a nightmare."

The bikers broke out laughing.

"She's all hooched up," one said. "You can't have no fuckin' nightmare when you're awake."

"You're losing your fuckin' mind, dude," said Schuyler as she led her out.

Rachel could have died of embarrassment.

"Hey, Rache," A shrill voice brings her back to the present.

It is a woman she met at one of the anti-fracking rallies. She doesn't want to be rude so she doesn't correct her about the torturous "Rache" nickname. She is with three other anti-frackers and they crowd in front of her bench, asking how she has been and why they don't see her at their meetings anymore.

"You in trouble with the law?" asks one of the male anti-frackers jokingly.

"Not me; someone else," she says, but does not elaborate.

She is surprised that they don't know about the case. After all, it was in the *Athens News* three months ago when the lawyers were arguing about plea bargains and shield laws and voir dire this or that. Well, her name was never mentioned. Throughout the newspaper report, she was referred to as "the alleged victim." Perhaps they are not aware she is the "alleged victim" which is rather amazing because gossip spreads like a forest fire in this county.

They tell Rachel they are attending a pre-trial hearing for one of their members charged with aggravated trespassing after chaining himself in front of an injection-well site in Albany. There has been a lot of activity since Rachel deserted them and they believe they are making some headway against fracking companies, they tell her.

"Come back. We need you," says one of the men, as they walk to the courtroom.

"And Skye Riley asks about you whenever he visits," says the woman.

"He knows my address and my phone number," says Rachel.

They had to bring up Skye Riley. She does not want to think of Skye Riley. Not since he started featuring in her nightmares. He featured twice actually, and on both instances, he just stood there looking at her pitifully. Then he slowly morphed into a smiling Jason. And back into Skye Riley again. No one said anything. Just the images morphing and re-morphing. Since then, the very thought of Skye has conjured up images of Jason. They have become the same person.

She is brought back from her reverie by Dylan Holton who tells her that the court is in recess after which she will be taking the stand as the first witness for the prosecution. He has brought her coffee in a Styrofoam cup. He does not say anything about the opening statements that were going on while Rachel waited outside.

After he had made his brief opening statement, which focused on the first-degree felony charge and the evidence that the state would present, Kayla Trenta went to town insinuating that this was not real rape. Evidence would be presented, she said, that the alleged offender was not a stranger but someone who was known to the alleged victim and had a relationship with her. The two were on a date that Christmas Eve, went for a drive the next morning, had drinks and some pot, and as two consenting adults had sexual relations. This first-degree felony charge against her client was unfortunate—result of a lovers' quarrel. Holton does not say anything about his own doubts after Trenta's spirited address that the prosecution's evidence is so weak that it may not stand the onslaught of her cross-examination.

"Just tell the truth as you remember it," says Holton. "Don't try to be smart or anything. If you don't know or don't remember, don't guess the answer or invent what you think is an appropriate answer. Say straight out you don't know or you don't remember."

After the recess, Rachel takes the witness stand. As she takes the oath her eyes wander to the jury box. She can identify some of the people, Athens being such a small town. The bailiff takes his place against the wall. Rachel's eyes wander to the table in front of the bench. Jason is sitting there with Kayla Trenta and another young gentleman, Trenta's clerk. The two men are in black suits, white shirts and black neckties. Trenta is also in black and white, except for the jacket which is turquoise. You could have sworn all three are lawyers and there is no rapist among them, thought Rachel.

Jason is staring at her unflinchingly. She quickly averts her gaze to the floor where it will remain for most of Dylan Holton's direct examination.

Holton is gentle and lacks the histrionics that Rachel has seen in television courtroom dramas. She is surprised that the judge only asks one question, even then to clarify Holton's question in response to Trenta's objection that Holton was leading the witness.

Judge Stonebrook seems to be a very mild-mannered man who listens attentively without much to say, unlike her favorite Judge Judy who tells litigants how stupid they are and how smart she is compared to them. She came prepared to be lambasted by the judge for her stupidity in allowing herself to be raped. But here the judge is not even looking at her. He has shut his eyes as he listens. Rachel is slightly agitated as

Holton guides her through the events of Christmas Eve and then Christmas morning.

She chokes at the most violent moments of the narrative and casts a defiant look at Jason for the first time as if daring him to contradict her.

"Did you have a relationship with the accused?" asks Holton.

"No, sir," Rachel responds.

"You are addressing yourself to Your Honor," says Holton.

"No, Your Honor."

"Did you consent to have sexual intercourse with him?"

Her cheeks turn red. How dare Holton even suggest it? Was he not listening to the story she just told of how it happened? But she controls herself.

"No, sir, Your Honor."

Even before he takes his seat, Kayla Trenta is on her feet. Rachel can't help admiring her while wondering why such a beautiful and classy woman decided to make defending rapists her career choice. She walks towards the witness stand and smiles sweetly at Rachel. Holton shifts uncomfortably on his chair. He knows her tactics; her softy-softy concession-based cross-examination is meant to coax the witness into giving answers that support her case. Because she is allowed

to lead the witness, Holton fears she will lull the unso-
phisticated Rachel into supporting the theory she
advanced during opening statements that the sex was
consensual.

"How long have you known Jason?" she asks.

"Since high school," says Rachel.

"You dated in high school, didn't you?"

Rachel denies they ever dated. She is led to admit
that they went to the movies together, just the two of
them, on a number of occasions, and did what she calls
"hanging out" at various places of entertainment and
fast-food restaurants.

"And still you say you did not date? How do you
define dating?"

"I mean we were not boyfriend and girlfriend."

Trenta leads her to admit that to everyone's per-
ception, and to Jason's, they were dating. And that after
a number of years, their friendship resumed when he
returned to Athens. Rachel strenuously denies that it
was a "relationship" despite Trenta's persistent line of
question that is meant to force her to admit that it was.
Even to the squirming Holton her denials lack credibility as Trenta leads her to admit they spent a lot of
time together, busked together, and she got him a job
at the Community Center run by her grandmother so
that they could be close to each other.

Trenta asks her about the Christmas Eve party, particularly how she was dressed. It didn't register to her why Trenta wanted her to describe every detail of the attire and even what parts of her body were exposed. She adopts a gossipy demeanor when she asks about the red and white Santa underwear that showed publicly. Holton knows exactly where this is leading.

"I'm sure you got quite a few admiring glances," she says with a school-girlish giggle. "From the men, that is. What did Jason say about your itsy-bitsy Santa Claus costume?"

"He liked it," says Rachel.

Trenta giggles again, looking at Rachel with a naughty twinkle in her eyes.

"You were on a date on Christmas Eve," says Trenta in a matter-of-fact manner.

"It was not a date. We were just all there partying. He was not with me."

"And yet you went for an early morning drive with him on Christmas day?"

"It wasn't really a drive. We took my friend Schuyler home."

"Why was Jason driving your car?"

She says she was tired. She admits that when they returned they smoked marijuana together and drank some bourbon. She was not high though, or drunk, because she only had a sip and a toke.

"We've heard that before, haven't we? I didn't inhale," says Trenta, obviously not directing that statement to her but to the court. A few people in the gallery chuckle or giggle, and the bailiff demands silence. Holton objects to the line of questioning and the defense counsel's insinuations, but Stonebrook rules Trenta should continue.

Rachel looks at the jury box and sees nothing but skeptical eyes. She looks at the gallery and sees Genesis and his wife. They are in the midst of men in black suits, elders from his church. She feels so alone; none of her people are here. Schuyler couldn't make it on this most important day and Nana Moira made it clear right from the beginning that she would not be attending any of these hearings. Not only is she ashamed that her granddaughter cried rape on a family friend, she does not want Genesis to think she is supporting that. She even tried to make amends with Genesis's family by visiting Jason in jail. Rachel was angry when Nana Moira told her about the visit.

"You didn't attend a single day of the court hearings, yet you have time to visit Jason?" she asked.

"I'm an old woman—I can't be going to no court. Schuyler is there for you."

And then she told her how well Jason looked, his cheeks filled up and his face round. He just sat there and smiled at Nana Moira and thanked her for coming, and said, "I hope someone is looking after my compost." That was all he had to say.

Trenta harps on marijuana and bourbon, a combination that would affect even the most hardened sailor.

"And yet you say this didn't affect you in any way?" she asks, still maintaining her kindly smile.

"I didn't want to have any of that," says Rachel desperately. "I just wanted to go home."

"Now I want to ask you about Skye Riley," says Trenta.

The prosecutor stands up to object.

"Skye Riley has no relevance in this case," he says. "Ms Trenta is trying to circumvent the shield laws by bringing him up."

Judge Stonebrook calls for a recess and demands to meet both counsels in his chambers. He demands that Trenta explain why she thinks Skye Riley is relevant.

"She wants to bring the victim's sex history with Riley, and Your Honor already ruled against that," says Holton even before Trenta can answer.

"This has nothing to do with the *alleged* victim's sex history, Your Honor," she is glaring at the prosecutor as she drags and stresses *alleged*. "It has to do with the fact that the two lovers, Rachel and Jason, had consensual sex, after which they quarreled about Skye Riley who was also having a relationship with Rachel.

Because both were not in a state of sobriety, they fought. Rachel was on the losing side of that physical altercation and she decided to cry rape to get even. That's how Skye Riley is relevant to this case. Nothing to do with anybody's sexual history."

Back in the courtroom, Trenta indeed pursues that line of question. To Rachel's shock, her demeanor is now completely different. She is in Rachel's face, trying to confuse and discredit her. She is bent on showing the jury that what she is saying doesn't jibe with common sense. Her denials that there was ever any consensual sex and any quarrel about Skye Riley sound hollow. She was determined to be strong until now. She breaks into tears.

Trenta is, however, relentless. She wants to know why Rachel didn't report to the police, if she was raped as she claims. She leads her to admit that she is an intelligent girl with a high-school education. Excellent grades. Could have gone to any great college if she had chosen to. In other words, she is not an idiot. And yet, she doesn't call the police after being raped? She doesn't go to the doctor?

"I went to the doctor. The deputy took me to O'Bleness," screams Rachel.

"After how long? Was it not after one whole week? Why did you wait that long?"

She is piling these questions on her and Rachel cannot give the answer. "I don't know" is all she can say.

"You're raped, you don't go to the police, you don't go to the doctor, and you don't know? Huh!"

Rachel hates Kayla Trenta even more than Jason. What gives her the right to stand here judging her? Obviously she has never been raped. She needs one real good rape. She is no longer listening to her questions as she fantasizes the rape of Kayla Trenta. The perpetrator is Jason de Klerk. Right there in the consulting room or wherever lawyers meet their clients. He strangles her with his manacles and rapes the daylights out of her. Then we'll see what she has to say about that, says Rachel to herself.

"Why were you together . . . just the two of you . . . at the Center?"

"I don't know," she says. She decides that's going to be her answer from now on. The best way to deal with this evil woman is to be passive aggressive.

"You told Mr. Holton that for days you scrubbed your body. Why did you do that?"

"I don't know."

"Why didn't you go for emergency contraceptives? All hospitals are required by law, as a condition of receiving federal funds, to provide emergency contraceptives to raped women," says Trenta. She is obviously adding this bit of information for the benefit of the jury.

"I don't know," says Rachel. When she sees that everyone is looking at her as if she is an idiot, she adds, "I wasn't thinking right."

When Kayla Trenta is done with her, Rachel is a mess of tears and mucus. She is not sure which was worse—what she experienced with Jason or what she has just gone through with Trenta. Maybe the latter because it replayed the former in public. She was savaged, pillaged, and plundered by Trenta in daylight. For all the world to see.

The prosecutor does not see any point of a re-direct. He knows that if he tries to clear up some of the issues that came up in her cross-examination Trenta will re-cross. That's her style. She will re-cross and break Rachel down altogether. The state's case has tremen-dously weakened as things are.

Judge Stonebrook reminds everyone that the jury will not be sequestered; both counsel have indicated they have no problem with that. He then adjourns the court until the next day.

Emergency contraception? Who said anything about pregnancy? There is no pregnancy here. Only the dead weight.

All she wants is to sleep. She is in a daze, but she will nurse her trusty Ford Escort on Route 50, and then on county and township roads, until she gets home. Slowly. She hopes the State Highway Patrol won't stop her for driving far below the regulated speed. They better not fuck with her. She's in no mood for any more officialdom.

She curses aloud when she sees a strange minivan parked outside her trailer next to Nana Moira's GMC Suburban. Company is the last thing she needs right now. When she gets closer, she notices that it is a Dodge Caravan with Michigan numbers.

Her heart skips a beat when her eyes fall on Genesis and two of the church elders she saw in court sitting on her sofa. Nana Moira has just served them cookies and is brewing coffee for them. The men stand and tip their hats. Rachel says "hi" and then rushes to her room.

Blue is on the floor next to the dressing table. Rachel picks her up and holds her to her bosom. She lies on her bed and shuts her eyes. She does not want to think of the trial. It was a disaster. Kayla Trenta made even her believe she was the slut who cried rape.

She takes refuge in happier times. As far back as her memory can take her. To the days when her pops was up and about playing his guitar and filling the house with booming laughter. Those were the days when he brought her the enduring Amish doll. It is a happy memory. But something mars it. Some vague sadness impinges on it. Not today's sadness. She knows the source of today's sadness. Sadness of another time. Perhaps another place. Something about the game she played with her pops. She doesn't know what game it was exactly. Doesn't remember. But whatever it was, she didn't enjoy it. She endured it because she was playing it with her pops. And she loved her pops. He was her protector. She felt safe around him. She dreaded the game, but she missed her pops whenever he was away singing and telling his tall tales. She misses her pops now. If only he were here Jason wouldn't have done what he did and Genesis wouldn't be hounding her. She reprimands herself. Who said Genesis's visit has anything to do with her? He and Nana Moira have always been friends.

There is light tap at the door and Nana Moira enters.

"Damn, I should have locked," says Rachel. "I wanna rest, Nana Moira. I had a rough day."

"Yeah, that's what Genesis tells me."

"So, he came to gloat?"

"The visitors wanna talk to you."

"They're not my visitors."

"You can't be rude to visitors, Rachel. You can't be rude before you hear what they wanna say to you."

Rachel covers her head with a pillow, but Nana Moira snatches it away and throws it on the floor.

"If you don't come out, I am gonna ask them to come in here," she says as she walks out of her room.

Rachel is left with no choice but to join the visitors in the living room.

The men greet her in polite hushed tones and ask her to be comfortable because what they want to discuss with her is to her advantage. They have nothing against her, they assure her. She is a child of God like all folks in all of creation and they are interested in her welfare. It's the duty of every Christian to forgive, so they forgive her for the pain she has caused both Nana Moira and Genesis.

"Christ said we should forgive seventy times seven," says one of the elders.

"That's a lotta times," says Nana Moira, cackling away. "We got a lot of forgiving before we're done."

No one else is laughing.

Rachel stares at the visitors defiantly. She has endured a lot of crap from Kayla Trenta. She is not about to endure more crap in her own house.

"From what we heard today in that man's court my boy's gonna walk," says Genesis.

"So it's time to think about the future," says the elder.

"I've no future with Jason," says Rachel.

"Obviously you don't," says the other elder. "Not after lying like that about him."

Genesis and the first elder shush him. They don't want to create a hostile environment here. This woman should not be alienated at all costs.

"We're talking about the child," says Genesis.

"Genesis's grandchild."

"I wanna take all responsibility for the child," says Genesis. "I'll give it everything it needs. I want that child to take my name, de Klerk. I want to give it learning and all the religious upbringing and the healthcare it needs. I got awful good insurance, not Medicaid."

"What Genesis is saying is let's bury the hatchet and think of the interests of the child," says the elder.

Rachel waits until they are all done with laying out their plans for the child before throwing the grenade.

"There's no child," she says gleefully.

"There's no child?" screams Nana Moira.

"Nana Moira told me you're with child," says Genesis.

"It's dead. Dead!" says Rachel, and laughs at their despondence. Now she is having a great time.

"What does she mean the child is dead? Did she . . . did she . . . ?" The elder can't bring himself to utter the word "abortion."

He is staring at Rachel's belly which is protruding a little.

"She must have," says Nana Moira.

"Is that not what you wanted Nana Moira? Is that not what you and Schuyler encouraged me to do?"

All eyes turn on Nana Moira.

"In the beginning, yes. But I didn't know Genesis was gonna want the child for himself. I didn't know his boy was gonna walk. And Rachel told me she didn't go through with it."

The men say they don't have any more business here and depart. At the door Genesis gives Nana Moira a look that says "I'm very disappointed in you" before he exits.

Rachel is pleased with herself. It is a small victory, but it is worth savoring after all the defeats, including the biggest one today.

"You shamed us, Rachel," says Nana Moira. "Why didn't you tell me you done it?"

Rachel gets Cheetos from the cupboard and starts crunching.

"You lied about the baby, didn't you? You lied to the visitors?"

"I didn't lie. The baby is just dead weight in my body. It was just something awful growing in me. I hated it so it died. It'll flush itself out. That's all I'm waiting for now. It has no name. It is nothing."

"God will punish you, Rachel."

"Why? Because I did it my way, not yours? You know nothing about God, Nana Moira."

"It's against the Bible what you're doing to Genesis and his unborn grandchild. My great-grandchild too."

Rachel's guffaws are mirthless and mocking. As far as she can remember, Nana Moira has never been to church except for an odd wedding or funeral, yet she is so unscrupulous as to bandy the Bible about whenever she wants to have her way. She never cites any chapter or verse, just the name of the book itself. Some vague notion of biblical injunction.

"Don't you threaten me with the Bible. Where was the Bible when I was raped?"

She has made up her mind—she will not go to court again. After the humiliation at the hands of Kayla Trenta she would not be able to withstand the gazes and the sniggers—real or imagined. Anyway, it's not her business. It is the State against Jason de Klerk, and the prosecutor told her that her only role is that of a witness. Like Jason raped the State and she was only a passer-by who witnessed the act. They can keep their trial.

She is not there to hear the evidence of the deputy who arrested Jason. The suspect denied having sex with the alleged victim. Of his free will he made a statement to that effect. The witness stands his ground when Trenta suggests that her client made the statement under duress. She had tried to persuade the judge in a previous hearing to declare the statement inadmissible, but failed.

For this witness there is a re-direct and a re-cross. Holton wants to impress on the jury that Jason, from the time of arrest, has been insisting that there has been no sex between him and Rachel, that he was the first to leave the Center after dropping Rachel there, and that he did not know what happened to her afterwards. He brazenly stuck to this story because he knew that Rachel had taken many baths after the rape, washing away any evidence. He only changed his story to consensual sex after his counsel learned via the discovery process of the existence of DNA evidence. In Jason's first version there was nothing about spending time with Rachel, drinking and smoking marijuana. He said he drove in with Rachel, left Rachel in her car, went to his, and drove away.

Rachel is not there to see Schuyler sitting in the gallery or to witness the glimmer of hope on Holton's face during the evidence of the doctor who examined her a week after "the alleged rape." Rachel had a tear on the vagina on the mend and bruises on her face, between her thighs, and on other parts of her body. Trenta makes a show of suggesting through her leading questions that all these do not prove rape. When her client takes the stand he will give evidence that he and Rachel engaged in rough sex, demanded by *her*.

Consensual aggressive sex comes up again when she cross-examines the expert who testifies to the presence of Jason's DNA on the traces of semen on the floor, some of which was mixed with blood proved to be Rachel's after tests. This is crucial evidence for the prosecution; it was after this discovery that Jason changed his story from no sex to consensual sex.

Rachel is pub-crawling on Court Street when the prosecution rests its case and the lawyers argue in front of Judge Stonebrook, but in the absence of the jury, over the evidence. Trenta is asking for a motion to demurrer, an immediate plea for dismissal due to lack of evidence, and Holton is vigorously opposing it. The judge rejects the motion.

Rachel is being refused service at Tommy's and passes out on a chair when the jury is called in and the defense begins its case. Jason de Klerk takes the stand and insists the sex was consensual. "We was just sitting there conversating and drinking and smoking," he says. Then they fell into each other's arms and kissed and made love. Rachel demanded that he be faster and rougher. The prosecutor's cross-examination harps on his previous statement that there was no sex. He says he lied because he was scared. The deputy threatened him, he adds.

"Why do you imagine Rachel accuses you of rape after having a good time with you?" asks Holton.

"I don't wanna imaginate nothing like that."

Obviously he has forgotten the story his attorney already advanced to Judge Stonebrook in chambers that after intense lovemaking there was a quarrel about Rachel's relationship with Skye Riley. But Trenta forces him to recollect and recount the story in her re-direct.

There are no other witnesses. Trenta very much wanted to call Moira Boucher as Jason's character witness. She refused. Much as she liked the boy and felt sorry for Genesis, she would not stand in a witness box against her own granddaughter, and she told Genesis and later an investigator sent by Trenta so. Trenta could easily have subpoenaed her but she didn't want a hostile witness in her hands.

The defense rests and the prosecution says it will not call any rebuttal witnesses. Both counsel are ready with their closing statements.

Trenta dwells at length on Jason's hard work and dedication to the Center, his love for music and for

Rachel, his being cuckolded by Skye Riley, his being led on by Rachel on Christmas morning until they had sex, his fear when the deputy arrested him while working at the Center, and his unfortunate statement, a result of that fear, that there was no sexual intercourse between him and Rachel.

Holton's remarks are brief and focus on the reliability or lack thereof of the witnesses. The accused made, of his free will and after being warned of the consequences, a false statement under oath, to the sheriff.

"In rape cases usually it is the word of the alleged victim against that of the alleged perpetrator. None of us were there. We can only depend on whose story has credibility . . . who is more of a reliable witness. Rachel Boucher has been consistent in her story. It is supported by DNA evidence on the floor, which Ms Trenta rightly points out only establishes there was sexual intercourse, and does not prove there was rape. But we remember that the accused denied in his sworn statement that there was any sexual intercourse at all. It was only after he discovered the presence of this DNA evidence that he changed his story to consensual sex. He has lied before, how can we be sure he is not lying now? He has no credibility at all. Ms. Boucher on the other hand has been credible and reliable in her evidence. The bruises she suffered all over her face and other parts of the body can only be the result of savage violence rather than so-called rough sex. Think about this, members of the jury, if sex between the two was consensual, why would Ms Boucher all of a sudden accuse the man of rape? Just because they quarreled about her boyfriend? It does not hold water, ladies and gentlemen."

Judge Stonebrook gives his instructions to the jury and the court is adjourned.

Schuyler finds Rachel at Tommy's and tells her the trial is over. They are waiting for the jury's verdict.

"I don't give a fuck about any fucking trial," says Rachel. "I just wanna go home and sleep."

But they can't find her car. It's been towed away because it was illegally parked the whole day. Schuyler drives her friend home in her pick-up.

It takes all of three days for the jury to come out. This is a sign to Genesis that his son will not be convicted. The worst that can happen is a mistrial. He is indeed vindicated when the jury announces that it is deadlocked on the rape charge, but finds him guilty of a lesser crime of assault, a first-degree misdemeanor.

All members of the jury believe that Rachel and Jason were in a relationship, as he claims, and were on a date that night. But where they are deadlocked is whether the sex was consensual or not. Some members argued that from the evidence it was obvious to them that this was a case of date rape. Others swallowed

Jason's story that it was consensual rough sex. They all agreed that Jason acted recklessly and hurt the woman, hence the assault verdict.

Judge Stonebrook has no choice but to sentence Jason to six months' imprisonment, which would amount to time served, and a fine of one thousand dollars.

As Kayla Trenta walks out of the courtroom with Genesis and his entourage of Michigan church elders, he moans about the lack of justice in this whole matter. Trenta turns to him and sternly says, "Stop whining. I worked my butt off to save your son. You should be grateful he only got six months. For rape, people get life with no possibility of parole."

Rachel is languishing at home when Schuyler comes with the report of the sentence. She doesn't care, she says. She is, however, really annoyed when she hears that they concluded she was on a date with Jason.

"I wasn't on a date with him," she yells.

She can do with a beer right now. But since her car was towed away and is impounded she has been confined to home. And there are no buses between Jensen Township and the city. Schuyler is always busy with her "own things," whatever that means, and Rachel doesn't see her as much as she used to. Rachel is like a prisoner, with only Nana Moira for company in the evenings.

7

Rachel's Blue. He is radiant like a lilac despite the fact that his mother did not have any prenatal care during her pregnancy. He lies in a cot next to his mother's bed. She spends hours just staring at the sleeping miracle. The gaze continues when the miracle is awake, holding a rattle tightly in his little hand and singing *dah*, *dah*, *dah* to the percussive rhythm.

Against all predictions, there are no signs of fetal alcohol syndrome. He was full-term and weighed all of eight pounds at birth. His eyes don't have the narrowness of FAS babies. They are wide and bright, gleaming with warmth. No thin or flat upper lip. No tremors, shaking, irritability, or diarrhea. Perhaps the final weeks that the mother spent in a state of sobriety helped. The baby went cold-turkey while still in the womb and completed the withdrawal cycle. Perhaps the fact that she only started her heavy drinking after the first trimester also contributed to the miracle. Rachel is not going to waste her time exploring reasons. She is only happy that all the township gossip, fueled by Nana Moira, was off the mark. Her Baby Boy Blue is normal and lovable.

"Your baby's gonna be the village idiot 'cause you drink like a fish," Nana Moira used to tell her when she came home drunk. When she stayed home because she was broke, Nana Moira said it was good for the child. In both instances Rachel told her, with much sadistic pleasure, the child lived only in her grandma's imagination. In her womb there was nothing but dead weight.

It was an arduous road that took Rachel from "the enemy within" to "dead weight" to a "baby girl" and finally to a bouncy baby boy. It started with a kick. She had been sober for weeks when it happened. Her sobriety was not by choice. For a while she didn't have a car to drive to the bars of Athens. Even after she had pawned some of her stuff, including her guitar, and released her car from impound, she still was unable to feed her habit. Nana Moira had wised up and was not giving her any of her money to mess up her life with, not even for gas. It was summer and the city was devoid of horny students who'd buy her beer for a roll on the backseat of a car at some parking lot. She was on her uppers, so she stayed home and discovered that she actually loved waking up without a hangover. And without the guilt, followed by long showers during which she exfoliated the skin that rubbed against the bodies of strange men.

Schuyler didn't visit often because she now had a job as a receptionist for Mr. Troy, the lawyer who defended her when she had stolen her boyfriend's ashes. Perhaps she also was beginning to despair with her friend and the way she was bent on destroying her life. She tried to talk her into getting a job at any of the fast-food outlets in town instead of spending the whole day sleeping and watching daytime television and then sleeping again.

None of them mentioned the dead weight in her belly. Until all three women conveniently forgot its existence.

The kick happened on a day like any other. She was in bed with Blue, after a breakfast of grits and milk. She had covered her head in her comforter and was listening to Power 105 on her cell-phone radio. She felt a mild kick.

"Hey, Blue kicked me," she said. She had taken to talking aloud to herself since she was the only company she had. She also talked to Blue.

There was another kick after a minute or two. This one more forceful. She jumped up and held her belly. She could feel more movement. The dead weight had risen from the dead. It was moving inside her. Not in a manner she imagined an "enemy within" would move—crudely and roughly and excruciatingly. But in motions that were smooth and flowing like water in a creek. They made her want to laugh. A violent kick sent her into giggles as she caressed her belly. Titillating violence.

"Baby Blue is kicking me!" she said.

When Nana Moira arrived in the evening, Rachel announced: "Blue is restless tonight."

Nana Moira did not pay any attention to her. She was packing the canned food she brought from the Center.

"I'm going to keep Blue, Nana Moira," said Rachel.

"Of course I won't hide Blue again," says Nana Moira absent-mindedly. "Nobody'll do nothing to your Blue."

Rachel is bubbly beyond words and Nana Moira stops to look at her.

"I'm talking about the baby I'm carrying. I'm going to keep it."

Nana Moira breaks out cackling.

"The one you called dead weight? And before that you called it an enemy."

"It's not dead anymore. It's kicking like crazy in me."

"So you call it Blue?"

"I call *her* Blue. She's a beautiful baby girl."

Perhaps it was the only way Rachel could accept the baby, thought Nana Moira. She would therefore play along and call the baby Blue. Only until the baby is born. After that it will have a real name like all Bouchers.

Everyone just took for granted that Blue was a girl. The name itself led them in that direction. They could not imagine a boy named Blue. The "Little Boy Blue" nursery rhyme did not come to mind.

"She had a restless night," Rachel would say after Blue had been kicking and boxing in her belly.

The original Blue lay forgotten on the dressing table.

The next day Nana Moira came home early. She had brought some yarn and knitting needles from Wal-Mart and sat on the sofa with Rachel, teaching her how to knit. At first Rachel was resistant because she didn't think she had the knack for it, but she soon got into the spirit of things. The first bootee she knitted looked like a bird's nest. After three or so attempts, her fingers got less jittery and her creations looked more like store-bought bootees. The following days she would be immersed in knitting pink, white, and yellow bootees, caps, and rompers.

"It's cheaper to buy this stuff from thrift stores than to knit it yourself," said Schuyler once when she came visiting.

"Don't pay her no never mind," said Nana Moira. "The Boucher women are never lazy to do stuff with their own hands for their young-uns."

"I do it because I like it," said Rachel. "Plus it keeps me busy. Plus Blue will wear something her mom made."

It was the first time she used the word "mom" in relation to herself. Nana Moira knew she had reached a point of no return. She could even give her money to buy stuff in town without fearing that she would take a detour to some Court Street bar.

The kick also brought a new sparkle in Rachel's eyes. Color returned to her cheeks. She began to enjoy food instead of just following the motions of eating in order to stay alive. She even had respite from nightmares. She believed that Blue had kicked them away.

She was bubbly right up to the time the baby was born. When her water broke, Nana Moira did not drive her to O'Bleness Hospital or anywhere else. Instead, she called Missy Cline, the township-community midwife, to do the honors.

Nana Moira has known her for ever, from the days when Missy Cline was a young lay midwife who helped bring Rachel to the world. She has presided over the birth of many babies in Jensen Township, especially in the days when home births were more common.

When business became slow with many folks opting for O'Bleness or Holzer because they had insurance or Medicaid coverage, she had to up her game; she studied more, wrote exams, and got certified by the North American Registry of Midwives.

Nana Moira said all the Boucher children, from the beginning of time, were born at home because they were no pansies. They all grew up to be strong men and women without any of the diseases that one gets from a hospital. They were not given any of the cockamamie immunization either, until the school system forced them to. In any event, a community midwife was more convenient and cheap, especially because Rachel had not gone through the Medicaid application process for prenatal care, labor and delivery, and postpartum care.

"Just like folks raise organic food in these parts, the Bouchers have always raised organic babies," said Nana Moira as Missy Cline was busy preparing Rachel's bedroom for the delivery.

"Back in the day there was nothing organic 'cause everything was organic," said Nana Moira, now following Missy Cline as she helped Rachel walk around the room. "We didn't know a damn thing about that word neither."

Missy Cline only mumbled her concurrence as she walked Rachel to the toilet. She asked her to sit down and pee or do number two if she could. Then she led her to take a walk outside. All the while, Nana Moira came hobbling after them with her walking stick and telling Rachel she would have made things easier for everyone if she had not started by talking of dead weight but had asked Missy Cline to help with the pre-natals. Rachel told her grandma to shut up.

"You don't wanna cause tension, Nana Moira," said Missy Cline. "It's gonna slow down the girl's labor."

"I'm not a girl," said Rachel.

"To us you are," said Nana Moira.

"Make her some coffee instead," said Missy Cline. "Or maybe warm milk."

She led Rachel back to the bedroom when she felt some contractions.

"You better hurry popping that baby," Nana Moira said to Rachel, before hobbling to the kitchen. "We don't have all day."

"You allow the baby to take its own time, Nana Moira," said Missy Cline. "It gotta set its own pace. You don't rush no birthing."

And indeed the baby did come when it was ready, after a whole day of labor that Rachel endured with fortitude. Now she was screaming and asking for what-ever drugs that could stop the pain.

"We do it all natural, honey," said Missy Cline. "We don't use no drugs."

Nana Moira was jittery herself, and Missy Cline was trying to calm her while also attending to Rachel. The midwife urged Rachel to adopt any position in which she felt comfortable; she could lie on the side or squat or kneel or whatever.

"I'm getting outta here," Nana Moira said all of a sudden. She was getting tense.

"Don't you wanna catch the child when it's born?" asked Missy Cline. "Usually relatives catch the child as it comes out."

"I don't wanna see any birthing. It's an ugly and disgusting thing to see."

Missy Cline could not help laughing. After all, Nana Moira had given birth before, and was present at births of relatives, including Rachel's.

"But I never looked," said Nana Moira.

"So you won't be of any help? What good are you then?"

Rachel screamed that they should stop arguing and attend to her.

"You catch the baby yourself," said Nana Moira. "Then give it to me. Don't give it to Rachel before you give it to me. I must touch it first."

All three women knew why she wanted to touch it first. The baby adopts the personality of the person who is the first to touch it after birth. That's the whole idea of having a relative with a wonderful personality catch it as it comes out.

"But I'll have touched it first," said Missy Cline. "Sure you don't wanna change your mind and catch the baby?"

"You're no relative so it won't adopt your personality," said Nana Moira.

"It doesn't say the first relative to catch it," said Missy Cline. "It says the first person."

"Just give it to me before you place it on Rachel. We don't want nothing of Rachel in this baby's personality, we don't want this baby to be running around with the likes of Schuyler getting herself in all sorts of trouble like her mama did. The baby will have my great personality."

The midwife caught the baby. After making sure it had no breathing difficulties, she gave it to Nana Moira to touch just for a few seconds before placing it on Rachel's stomach for instant bonding. She instructed Rachel to put it immediately on the breast because that would reduce her bleeding and stimulate the uterus to contract. It would also give the baby some colostrum to fight bacteria and build up the baby's immune system.

The first thing that Rachel noticed was the little weenie.

"My baby Blue is a boy," she cried. And then she laughed.

So was the journey from dead weight to a boy named Blue.

Genesis hears of Blue from people who heard the midwife boast to friends of yet another successful delivery. He drives to the Center and demands to talk to Nana Moira. It is one of the busiest days of the month, with dozens of people lining right up to the gate for food parcels. Their beat-up automobiles fill the parking lot and spill into the street, making a long line there. Nana Moira sits at the table ticking the names while two volunteers are putting together a parcel of canned vegetables, flour, powdered milk, rice, cabbage, sugar, coffee, and other items of grocery. They all place these in a plastic bag before handing them to the client.

"No time for powwow, Genesis," says Nana Moira. "See all those folks out there?"

"I just wanna know why you didn't tell me about the baby," says Genesis.

"Shush, you can't talk about our business in public," says Nana Moira.

She orders him to sit down and help with the food distribution instead.

"I got work of my own," says Genesis.

"Your cheese is not running anywhere, Genesis. Sit down and put in an honest day's work, after that you gonna tell me what you're all whining about."

He reluctantly takes a seat and watches the volunteers pack the food and give the parcel to the next person on the line and Nana Moira ticking the name on the list.

"I've a friend who's got eggs," says Genesis after a while.

"Your friend lays eggs, big deal," says Nana Moira, and breaks out cackling.

"Don't bullshit me now, Nana Moira. You know what I'm talking about. He can give you plenty eggs."

"I don't need eggs," says Nana Moira.

"These folks need eggs. I don't see any protein here. Only canned beans. They need more than that."

This gets Nana Moira interested. But she still does not take Genesis seriously. She can't see how and why anyone could donate eggs to feed all the needy folk in the community—by all reckoning, two-thirds of Jensen Township.

"If you cooperate with me about the baby I can get my bud to give you plenty eggs."

Once more Nana Moira breaks out laughing. She is even more amused by Genesis's perplexed look. He is obviously trying to figure out what is funny about his offer.

"You wanna buy the baby with eggs?" asks Nana Moira, which causes mirth to the volunteers and the clients who are front in line and were pretending not to be listening to what is clearly not their business. Genesis looks sheepish as he stands up to leave.

"Come back later," she calls after him. "We'll talk. It's gonna take us all day to dole out this food."

"I won't allow you to make a laughing stock of me, Moira Boucher," he says as he exits.

Later in the afternoon Genesis is back. Although Nana Moira is not done for the day, she decides to lock up. They drive in Genesis's truck to Rome Township where his friend raises hens for eggs.

"You and Rachel lied to me, Nana Moira. You said there was no baby," says Genesis as he negotiates the twists and turns on CR 329.

"I didn't. Rachel said so. She lied to me too."

Then why didn't she notify him when she discovered it was a lie? Nana Moira has no answer for that, except to confess that it has been difficult to deal with Rachel since the rape. Her moods change and sometimes it is impossible to understand what she wants.

"There was no rape, Nana Moira, you know that," says Genesis.

"She says there was," says Nana Moira.

"You know my boy can't rape anyone, so let's not hear of this rape crap anymore."

They drive silently for a while. And then Genesis says, "I told Revelation about the baby. He wants to take full responsibility."

"And that's a good thing too," says Nana Moira. "But how'll he do it since he disappeared and no one's seen him since he walked out of that darn court a free man?"

"I see him all the time. He's in Michigan where no folk judge him like they do here. And he's found God too. He's training to be a lay preacher of the church."

"Good for him," says Nana Moira.

The chicken farmer is happy to finally meet Nana Moira. He says he has heard from Genesis and others of the great work she is doing running the Jensen Community Center. He takes them to meet his egg-layers. Nana Moira expected to see battery cages and scruffy white hens imprisoned in them. But here are hundreds of hens running free in a fenced-in field, scratching for food in the green grass. They come in all colors, shapes, and sizes, just like backyard chicken. The farmer says he feeds them corn and greens and whatever else they can scratch for themselves. This makes their eggs very tasty. They are free to roam about and go in and out of the henhouses at the edge of the yard as they please.

"How many dozens do you want?" he asks.

"We don't have money to pay for eggs," says Nana Moira. "Whatever we get from donors goes to the Food Bank in Logan."

"Didn't Genesis tell you? I'm donating them."

She just wanted to make sure, she says. She always wants to put her cards on the table for everyone to see.

"Forty dozen," she says and breaks out cackling. She thought she was being ridiculous, and everyone would laugh at the joke. But no one laughs. Instead the farmer says, "I'll give you eighty dozen every two weeks."

This almost floors her. Eighty dozen? How can he afford to give out so much for free?

"You don't look at a gift horse," says Genesis.

"You don't?" asks Nana Moira.

The farmer tells her that in fact he can afford to donate one hundred and twenty dozen. He gives the rest to children's homes and nursing homes in the city. If he was not donating them to somebody he would have to dump them. He cannot sell all the eggs he produces to Wal-Mart and other formal markets. After collecting them from the henhouses, he runs them through a machine that grades them, separating them according to size and weight. Those that have different coloration or are too small or too large to fall into the four categories—medium, large, extra-large, and jumbo—cannot be sold to retailers. He sells some of them directly to the public at the farmers' market instead, and donates the rest to the needy. He has been donating eggs to food pantries all over southeast Ohio, but since he is an admirer of Genesis and of the work that he hears Nana Moira is doing for the community, he might as well make a regular donation of eighty dozen eggs to the Jensen Community Center. He says this with a flourish, and both Nana Moira and Genesis cheer and applaud.

When Nana Moira returns home she is in a cheerful mood.

"We gonna have eggs," she says. "Thanks to Genesis we gonna have eggs."

"Shush," says Rachel, "you'll wake up Blue."

Nana Moira tells her granddaughter that Genesis says the de Klerk family wants to take full responsibility of Blue. She puts it that way because she knows if she says Jason wants to take full responsibility, she will go all hysterical on her.

"What do they mean they want to take full responsibility?"

"Child support, maybe. He didn't say. He just said full responsibility."

"Tell him I don't want their support."

"Beggars cannot be choosers," says Nana Moira.

Rachel knows exactly what she means. She is unemployed and depends on SNAP. However, since they get all their food free from the Food Pantry, she is able to convert the food stamps under the table for diapers, formula, and other items she needs for the baby. Nana Moira also contributes something from her meager stipend. Despite her penury, she will not accept anything from the de Klerk family.

It is for the good of the child to have a strong and respected family like Genesis de Klerk's on its corner, Nana Moira tells her. That will assure its future.

"This baby won't eat your pride. It won't get schooling from it."

Rachel has her whole life ahead of her and she doesn't want the encumbrance of a baby while she is mapping out her future, adds Nana Moira. Since she failed to abort Blue, maybe she should seriously consider giving him up for adoption. What better family can one think of as the home of a baby in the whole of southeast Ohio than the de Klerks?

"Now they wanna adopt my baby?"

"They didn't say that. I'm just saying. Give them a chance, Rachel."

Nana Moira is in the kitchen at the Center cooking bean soup with bones for lunch. She can hear snatches of the gossip of the Quilting Circle women. They miss Jason, they say. He was a great guy, very kind and considerate. Very funny too. Now he is languishing somewhere in Michigan because some unscrupulous woman concocted lies about him. But the truth is coming out; everyone can see that she was not raped. There is no rape victim who would want to keep the baby of the rapist.

Nana Moira is now standing at the door and doesn't like what she hears, even though it became clear to her the moment Rachel failed to go through with abortion that she would be viewed with suspicion for keeping the child.

"She's still my granddaughter, you don't talk of her like that," says Nana Moira, her arms folded on her chest.

The women fall silent. But there is one who feels that the truth must be told, even if it does not sit well with their mentor. And she says so.

Genesis saves the situation when he arrives with Wal-Mart plastic bags full of baby stuff. Diapers, rompers, bootees, baby oil, baby powder, and the like. There are "oooh"s and "aaah"s as the women admire them. The outspoken woman feels vindicated. Jason and her father are men of integrity. What woman would not want to belong in a family like this?

Nana Moira cannot wait for the evening to see Rachel's face when she receives the gift. She drives home right away and finds Rachel hanging out with Schuyler and Blue. Nana Moira had not seen Schuyler for some time and was pleased that her friendship with Rachel was cooling off a bit. Her face cannot hide her displeasure at seeing Schuyler back in Rachel's life.

"I thought you said your friend now has a job. Why's she here?" asks Nana Moira.

"You can ask me, Nana Moira, I am here," says Schuyler.

"I can see you're here. That's why I'm asking why."

She didn't feel like work today so she called in sick. She would rather spend the day with her friend, Rachel, and her Baby Boy Blue. Anyway, work is boring at Mr. Troy's office and she just can't get the hang of it. Rachel says that's how she lost her previous job; she pretended to be sick so many times they got sick of her, while she was gadding about with her biker boyfriend.

Nana Moira gives the plastic bags to Rachel but does not tell her that they are from Genesis. Rachel assumes they are from Nana Moira and she thanks her profusely and kisses her. Schuyler says she is fortunate to have a grandmother who cares for her even though that same grandmother can be full of crap sometimes.

The following Sunday the elders of Genesis's church descend on Rachel's double-wide. There are five of them in black suits, and there is Genesis in his regular red-and-white plaid shirt and dirty jeans. He is not one for dressing up even for church, from which they have all returned.

Rachel and Blue are in the bedroom when the visitors arrive, but she knows exactly who they are when she hears their voices.

"I was afraid your granddaughter would stay away for the day if she knew we were coming," says Genesis in response to Nana Moira's complaint about the unannounced visit.

"Genesis just wants to see his grandson," says one of the elders.

Nana Moira hollers that Rachel should bring the baby because Genesis wants to see him. Rachel does not hesitate. She comes out with the baby, but keeps him in her arms as she stands in front of the elders.

"What's his name?" asks one of the elders.

"Blue," says Rachel.

They all cry "Blue?" in unison.

"What kind of name is that?" asks an elder.

"He'll need a proper name from the Bible," says another elder.

"Revelation," says Genesis.

"Revelation?" asks Nana Moira.

"From Genesis to Revelation," says Genesis.

"But we gave that one to Jason," says the elder.

"The baby can always be Revelation Junior."

"Revelation Junior?" said an incredulous Nana Moira.

All this while Rachel's amazed gaze move from one speaker to the next. Nana Moira cannot contain herself. She breaks out cackling. The elders all look at her, and then at one another with questioning eyes. No wonder this girl is flighty—her grandmother is cuckoo. It's a pity that Jason had to sow his wild oats in a family like this.

"We want these two families, the de Klerks and the Bouchers, to come together and reconcile for the sake of the baby," says one of the elders.

"Let me hold him," says Genesis.

Rachel hesitates.

"Come on, Rachel, this is his grampa. He won't run away with Blue," says Nana Moira.

Rachel hands the baby over to Genesis.

"You call him that too?" asks Genesis.

"That's the name the mama calls her young-un," says Nana Moira. "It's no big deal—it's not permanent."

"It *is* permanent," says Rachel. "His name is Blue."

"It doesn't matter about the name for now," says an elder. "Let's talk business, in the interests of the child."

The elder outlines their plan. Genesis wants to adopt the baby. Although the elder is a lawyer, his practice is in Michigan. But he has looked at Ohio laws pertaining to adoption of rape-conceived children. As soon as he says this, Genesis and the other elders protest that Jason did not rape anyone.

Rachel is fuming inside. She indicates that she wants her baby back, but Genesis is engrossed in him, talking baby talk, telling him how smart he looks and that his grandpa will shower him with lots of pretty things.

"We know that," says the Michigan lawyer. "But the woman insists she was raped and that this is a rape-conceived child. What I am saying is the Ohio law facilitates adoption of rape-conceived children. This makes things easier for us. We can offer Rachel anything she wants, any amount of money."

"Blue is not for sale," Rachel says softly.

The lawyer adopts an avuncular mien and laughs. "You misunderstand me, Rachel. I'm not talking of buying a child. That would be absurd. You're still young. You still have a lot of life to live. We're talking of adopting your baby so that you're free to live your life. We'll pay for anything else that you want . . . college, if that's what you want . . . a career . . . a job. All that can be arranged. It will make you a better mother."

"It's not like you won't see the baby again," says Genesis. "It'll be next door here in Rome Township. You can visit any time you want."

"Give me my baby back," says Rachel, reaching for the baby resting contentedly in Genesis's arms.

"See how pretty he looks in the romper I bought him," says Genesis, as he makes to hand the baby to Rachel.

"That *you* bought him?" asks Rachel.

"Oh, no, oh no," says Nana Moira.

"Didn't Nana Moira tell you? I bought you plenty baby stuff."

Rachel snatches the baby and runs to her room. She lays the baby on the bed and takes out all the stuff Genesis bought. She is piling it on the floor when Nana Moira rushes in.

"You lied to me . . . again . . ." says Rachel, tears streaming down her cheeks.

"I didn't lie. I didn't say a thing."

The baby wants attention. It begins to cry. But Rachel takes no heed.

"You won't be wussing out of this now," says Nana Moira.

"I'm not wussing out. I was never in it in the first place."

Rachel rushes out of the room with all the items in her arms. Nana Moira wants to go after her, but decides to pay attention to the baby. She takes the baby and hobbles out to the living room where the elders are in various degrees of shock. Rachel gets kerosene from the lamp that is normally used when there are power outages and pours it on the clothes a short distance from the deck. The elders and Nana Moira, with Blue in her arms, all stand on the deck and watch her in horror as she sets the clothes alight. Even the baby oil and the baby powder go into the bonfire.

Rachel looks up at the elders and at Nana Moira and at Blue, and smiles. There is a beatific calmness about her. She can hear dark foreboding sounds in her head. Vague like the games her father played on her.

Nana Moira will not open the Center today. She is driving Rachel and Blue to the Tri-County Mental Health and Counseling Services because Rachel asked to be taken there. She fears that she is deteriorating to what she was when she still carried the dead weight. Even nightmares have returned. She can't afford to be in that state again. For Blue's sake she has to be well.

At the facility she is assigned a counselor.

It takes the professionals two other consultations before they are able to diagnose her—she has post-traumatic stress disorder. At first the counselor thought it was acute, but after a few more consultations she comes to the conclusion that it is chronic since it has persisted in excess of three months. She also has had relapses.

She is determined to fight this. For Blue's sake she will allow nothing to ever haunt her again.

8

Rain comes to Athens. She is one of the featured artists at a concert titled "An Evening of Appalachian Storytelling and Music." On the program she is a supporting act to an older balladeer by the name of Granny Sue from Shadyville, West Virginia.

Rachel is in the audience with three-year-old Blue. Rain is the only reason she is here. In the three years she has avoided any event that would take her back to her old life as a musician. Curiosity brought her here tonight. She remembered once a man called Skye Riley from the Blue Ridge Mountains telling her about his balladeer sister called Rain.

The Arts West auditorium is filled with the lovers of Appalachian folklore. Rachel was fortunate to get the front pew—the same one she remembers occupying with Schuyler almost four years ago when she first saw Skye riling up members of Appalachia Active. It seems so distant now. Another world. And sitting here with Blue, but without Schuyler, makes the memory even more poignant.

Schuyler. Rachel wishes she were here. But she can't be. She is doing time at a woman's penitentiary in another state.

Things got tough for her and the family when she lost her job with the lawyer Troy after missing many days of work. She really hated that job and just couldn't get the hang of it. So, she spent most of the day sitting on the porch with her brothers smoking blunts.

One day Schuyler asked Rachel out of the blue, "Have you ever thought of selling?"

Rachel wondered aloud where that question came from. Things were hard for her and Blue, but she had never thought of selling. She was making ends meet by knitting scarves that Nana Moira sold on her behalf to visitors at the Center—thanks to Nana Moira's lessons when she was pregnant with Blue. The returns were meager, but the thought of dealing in drugs had never entered her mind.

Rachel discovered that Schuyler bought herself a small digi-scale and a large bag of pot. She peddled it to construction workers revamping Route 33, thanks to Obama's stimulus. Schuyler assured Rachel there was nothing to worry about. She was only dealing in pot, nothing serious—no hard drugs.

Schuyler's business did not boom; she was a middle-man and was not making much profit. Her pool of regulars was small, and only once in a while did she get wildcard customers. Also she and her brothers used some of the weed themselves.

Rachel does not know how her friend got into meth. Schuyler's neighbors reported a strong chemical smell, almost like pee, coming from her house. Add to that the high volume of traffic—folks who came only for a few minutes and drove away. The law came calling one night, found meth-lab paraphernalia, and arrested every member of the family, including the parents. Although Schuyler took all the blame for the meth lab the rest of the family was charged—in Ohio it is a felony to fail to report a crime. The catch is that you must know it's a crime you're witnessing. The prosecution could not prove that the family knew what Schuyler was up to in her room, and the case against them was withdrawn.

Rachel remembers leaving Blue with Nana Moira and driving to Columbus to attend Schuyler's trial at the district court. She was determined to stand by her friend who had always been there for her when things were bad. Schuyler had a very good public defender who got her off with the minimum federal sentence of five years, despite her prior (remember the stolen ashes?). Since then Rachel has not seen her because she is serving her sentence at the Federal Correctional Institution in Danbury, Connecticut.

If Schuyler were here they would be laughing together at Thos Burnett's jokes and making silly remarks about his large Croc shoes and his broad tie on a blue denim shirt, with blocks of red, green, yellow, and blue, each block with a picture of Scooby-Doo in different poses. Thos is a famous storyteller in these parts, performing at fairs, zoos, festivals, and schools throughout Ohio, Indiana, and West Virginia. Rachel recalls that when she was a little girl, her pops took her to a reindeer farm in northern Ohio where for the first time she saw Thos telling stories. He was the resident storyteller at the farm.

Now here he is, much bigger and grayer, making Blue laugh his tummy sore with a story about Old Zach's dog that was cut into two by a blade of glass. Old Zach tried to sew it together. He only discovered when he was done that he had slapped it together in opposite directions—half of the head joined to half of the dog's ass. The dog could see from both ends and wag its tail likewise. The story got lost on Rachel as she marveled at Blue's relentless laughter. He was obviously following the adventures of Old Zach's dog in all their silly details. Rachel remembers her pops, like Thos Burnett an itinerant teller of tall tales. Once she had a dream to follow in his footsteps. She wondered why she abandoned a dream that would have filled folks with so much happiness.

The thought of her pops brings about a fleeting feeling of dread, an apprehension she doesn't understand. But she is also filled with a lot of joy that bubbles over to Blue. She finds herself embracing Blue tightly. He tries to free himself because she is breaking his concentration on the story.

It is Rachel's turn to be engrossed when Wormz and the Decomposers take the stage. The trio sings and plays variously the ukulele, the banjo, the guitar, and the mandolin. Rachel loves them most when they sing what they call "a dirty little song about water." Her fingers begin to itch as they pluck and strum invisible strings. A single tear runs down her face.

"Why you crying, mama?" Blue gives her a very concerned look.

"Because I'm happy, baby," Rachel says. "Very happy."

Finally the act she came here for takes the stage. Rain is introduced by the emcee, Thos Burnett, as Granny Sue's protégé. Rachel is struck by her calmness, her blond hair that cascades down her shoulders and her petite stature. She sings a cappella of the hills that bleed acid water from abandoned mines. Though Rachel is not much enamored with this style of ballading, she can identify with the words. Rain is singing of the same acid water that Rachel's Jensen community knows so well from their own bleeding hills.

After this Rain lunges into a ballad about "the man I loved more than anybody I ever knew," and then introduces Granny Sue.

It is obvious to Rachel that Granny Sue is well loved in these parts. Even as she walks onto the stage there is applause, whistles, and cheers. Rachel notices that she looks very much like an older and stouter version of Rain. The hair that cascades down her shoulders is white rather than blond. Rachel has seen Granny Sue's naughty smile and deliberate gestures on Rain. Clearly Rain sees herself as the heir to this great storyteller and balladeer.

"Now it's time for some storytelling and song making," says Granny Sue. "If you know anything about ballads they tend to sound like six o'clock news. All families tell stories. We all have those 'remember when' kinda stories. Like 'remember when grandpa fell down the stairs?' Calamity and mayhem make us laugh."

Then she begins to sing a ballad. Like Rain she sings a cappella. It is about a town that rises from the wilderness where there was nothing the previous day. Now in the night there are hotels and saloons and good-time girls lining the streets ready to entertain weary travelers. At the crack of dawn the town disappears again, only to emerge at nightfall. All the while, Rain is standing next to her, smiling and showing the appropriate facial expressions that the story demands.

And then they sing a duet—Rain and Granny Sue. It is nothing like harmony or unison. One singer sings a stanza and then relays the story to the next. The ballad is about a mine disaster and a young man who died there. It describes how handsome he was, then goes on to narrate how Number 8 was all flooded and all the men were doomed. The two balladeers sing the chorus "going down the dark hole" in unison.

Rachel is moved, but she thinks it would have been even better if they had arranged the whole ballad in soprano and alto harmony. That's how she would do it.

"If I had money these men would be checkers and whalers and not go down the black hole." The song continues to its end. After the applause, Granny Sue explains that in fact they would continue to go down the black hole because coal mining is their life, from the days of their great-grandfathers. Coal runs in their blood and they do not want to be anything else but coal miners.

"It's been like that with my folks," says Granny Sue. "It's been like that with Rain's folks. We live and eat and breathe coal."

By the time the concert ends, Rachel has decided she is going back to music. She will add storytelling and will travel like her father before her, and like Rain and Granny Sue, from place to place, bringing laughter and joy. One thing that strikes her most is that these storytellers and balladeers are folksy and country like her or Nana Moira or anyone else from her world, yet they all went to college from what she sees on the program. Thos Burnett has an MA from Bowling Green and is doing an MFA in storytelling from a university in Tennessee. Rain has an associate of arts degree from a community college in Kentucky. Even good old Granny Sue did a BS in education under the name Susanna Holstein at a West Virginia college.

"What stops me from being like these folks?" she asks herself as she pushes Blue in a stroller to the office at the back that is also used as a greenroom. She finds Rain and Granny Sue packing their stuff for the road back.

Rain's first reaction is to coo over the baby even before she greets the mom.

"Ain't she big for a stroller?" asks Rain.

"*He's* only three," says Rachel.

"Well, he's a cutie then. Could have sworn he's a girl," says Rain.

"At three he should be running all over the place. He needs the exercise," says Granny Sue.

"He gets plenty of it at home," says Rachel. "He's quite a handful running all over the place, like you say."

Rachel introduces herself and asks Rain if she is the same Rain that Skye told her about. She is indeed the same Rain. To Rachel's surprise, Rain knows something about her. She says her brother Skye used to talk about her a lot. Rain was almost certain that for the first time he was getting serious about someone because he never talked about the many flings he had at his anti-fracking campaigns.

"Now, you went and married someone else," says Rain.

"I didn't marry anyone," says Rachel.

She does not elaborate. Rain doesn't think it would be good manners to pursue the matter further. So they talk about music. And about storytelling. And they exchange contacts and promise to keep in touch.

Once more Rain comes to Athens. But this time not to perform for the public. She is visiting Rachel and has brought her a gift: an Epiphone acoustic guitar. It is green in color because a girl from the hills deserves a green guitar.

"I told Skye I met you," says Rain. "He wants to come and visit."

"I don't think that's a good idea," says Rachel. "And I hope this guitar is not from him 'cause I'm not gonna accept it."

Rain says she'll be very hurt if she doesn't accept it because she bought it herself with her meager savings after Rachel told her she used to sing and play but stopped more than three years ago when a man she used to play with did awful things to her. Rain thinks it has to do with lost love and warns Rachel never to let a man break her heart to the extent she gives up the one thing that matters in life—music. She bought her the guitar because Skye told her that Rachel's fingers were quite nifty on the strings and it would be a shame if she gave that all up because of some silly man. "But you can be rest assured," she says, "this guitar ain't from Skye. He knows nothing about it. It's from me. I want to hear you play."

Rachel approaches the guitar with some amount of trepidation.

"Come on, dude," says Rain. "Just play the darn thing. Make it squeal for its mama."

Rain reminds her so much of Schuyler. They called each other dude when they were happy or being naughty about something.

Rachel plays. Rain is wide-eyed and open-mouthed at the sophisticated way Rachel picks the notes and arpeggiates the chords. Rachel sings "Shady Grove, My Little Love" and Rain harmonizes in the chorus. It goes so well as if they had rehearsed together that they both break out laughing.

"Your voice is very nasally," says Rain.

"You and your brother have a way of insulting me," says Rachel, laughing nevertheless. "He once said my voice was whiny."

"He knows nothing what whiny means. It's nasally—that's what we call it. It can be annoying to some listeners. Some singers even try to correct it with surgery."

Rachel could easily have been irritated by this discussion. But she finds her guileless frankness refreshing. Rain tells her that she thinks it is silly to try to change ones voice through surgery. There is no need for voice coaches and speech–language pathologist either. She can use her voice to full effect as it is, as long as she uses a lot of comedy in her material. The voice lends itself well to comedy. It becomes part of the comic effect.

"Next time I've a gig worth my while I'll invite you over," says Rain. "We'll play together. It'll only take a few hours of rehearsal before the show for us to gel."

As she watches Rain drive away in her brown-and-white Volkswagen Beetle convertible, Rachel smiles and waves her goodbye with her guitar. Then she sits on the deck and plays and sings, defiantly making her voice even more nasally.

When Nana Moira returns home with Blue in the evening, Rachel is still playing her guitar.

Blue spends a lot of time with Nana Moira at the Center. She insists on taking him with her because, as she told Rachel once, "This young-un reminds me of you when you was his age." Rachel used to spend her days playing under the tables or on the porch and being spoilt by the Quilting Circle women with cookies and other goodies. It is now Blue's turn.

Before Rain came, Rachel and Nana Moira would fight over Blue. Nana Moira wanted to take him to the Center, Rachel wanted to play with him at home. But since the green guitar, Rachel is happy that she is able to practice and write new songs while Blue plays away at the Center.

She never used to write songs before but sang the standard folk songs that everyone from the hills knew. But now she is taking Rain's advice to heart; she has to come up with humorous material. Sometimes it's just her own funny words in old tunes, but once in a while, she comes up with an original ditty.

What she doesn't know as she strums her guitar is that Genesis has taken to visiting the Center at any odd moment just to see Blue. Nana Moira lets the two boys, as she calls them, play together on the porch or behind the building where Jason's compost lies abandoned and the wood that he split is still in a high pile. Nana Moira is pleased that Genesis is establishing some form of rela-tionship with his grandson. A boy child needs a man in his life, and what better man could one wish for as a role model than the upstanding Genesis?

These surreptitious visits have earned Genesis brownie points from the women of the Quilting Circle. He is a wonderful man who will not shirk his responsibility, they say. The visits have also earned Rachel more of the women's rancor. She is a heartless woman who has sent a good man away and now refuses the man's own flesh and blood to have anything to do with the man's father. She gives all women a bad name, they whisper out of the range of Nana Moira's hearing, and it is a good thing that she hasn't set her foot at the Center for years now.

Genesis does not tell Nana Moira that he consulted lawyers; he wants to have official visitation rights. He wants Revelation Junior, as he calls him, to spend some weekends with him at his house, breathing the clean fresh air and eating the wholesome vegetables that are cooked immediately after they leave the soil.

Genesis instructed his lawyer, who happens to be the same Mr. Troy that Schuyler worked for, to initiate court process for him and his wife to be granted visitation rights as grandparents. Troy advised him it would be a waste of money and effort because he didn't envisage winning that case. Yes, he could easily win a case for Jason's visitation rights as the natural father. But there is no pre-existing relationship between Genesis and the grandson—no bond of any kind exists between them—and therefore it would be impossible for Troy to argue in any Ohio court that visitation would be in the interest of the grandchild.

Could it be that Genesis is now trying to establish that bond?

On one of his visits, Genesis is sitting on the car seat at the porch with Blue on his lap. Nana Moira joins them with a bowl of mixed nuts. She passes it to Genesis who takes a few, throws one up and catches it with his mouth. He repeats the trick a number of times. Blue finds this very funny and laughs. He tries it too but can't catch the nuts. Genesis shows him how to do it, and on one instance, Blue manages to catch the nut. This is the source of laughter and high-fives.

"You can see he's a de Klerk through and through," says Genesis.

"Strange way of telling a de Klerk with catching nuts," says Nana Moira.

"He'll take the de Klerk name one day," says Genesis urgently. "He'll be Revelation de Klerk Junior. It's only natural."

"Well, he's registered as Blue Boucher on the birth certificate," says Nana Moira. "It's his mama's decision. Me and you don't have a thing to do with it."

"I have to talk to Rachel," says Genesis. "She must let this kid visit, even if it's just one weekend a month.

The kid gotta run wild and free in the farm like his daddy used to. You must do something about this Nana Moira."

Nana Moira tells him she has tried to talk sense into Rachel's head but she won't budge.

"Why has she got such a downright cranky disposition?" asks Genesis in frustration.

"You'd be cranky too if you was raped," says Nana Moira.

Genesis is taken aback. Nana Moira has surprised even herself with that statement.

"Now don't tell me you also believe that cockamamie bullshit that my boy raped her," says Genesis, putting Blue on the seat and standing up to face down on Nana Moira.

Nana Moira does not respond. She would rather not discuss Rachel. She knows about that "disposition." She has to deal with it every day. She also knows that in the last three years she has seen her granddaughter open up and bloom in a manner she had never witnessed before, even prior to the rape. Yes, she now does believe she was raped. Perhaps this counseling thing helps. Nana Moira never thought it would. She never believed there was any treatment for any ailment that could work without medicine or some kind of pill or injection. But Rachel has been going to the Tri-County Mental Health Services at least twice a month and all she does there is sit down with a counselor and talk. Just that. To Nana Moira's amazement, it has brought a lot of improvement in her temperament. That, and lately a woman called Rain who has brought music back in her life.

Nana Moira does not tell Genesis any of these things. She just sits there ruminating. She recalls how, one time, Rachel's counselor invited her for a session or two, with Rachel's permission. The woman made her feel so much at home that she found herself revealing a family secret she had never ever mentioned to anybody. Stuff—and that's what she keeps on calling the secret—that she saw happening when Rachel was a toddler. The disclosure came after she told the counselor that Rachel was a strange child even as she was growing up. The counselor probed more to find out why Nana Moira felt that way. Nana Moira felt safe and trusting, so she talked. Hesitantly at first, but the "stuff" came out.

The "stuff" confirmed what the counselor suspected all along, that Rachel's problem was more than the chronic PTSD or a rape-trauma syndrome as a result of the rape. She had suspected that Rachel was already vulnerable when she was raped by Jason. The counselor could identify signs of delayed-onset of PTSD, and Nana Moira's story about "stuff" confirmed her suspicions.

Nana Moira remembers how the counselor begged her to let Rachel know about the "stuff" because that would help in her healing, but Nana Moira said it would never be from her lips. She would not bear the shame. They left it at that. Well, Nana Moira left it at that, the counselor didn't. Once in a while she phones her and after some small talk asks if she hasn't changed her mind yet about letting Rachel into the secret.

Not only did those two sessions with the counselor make her reveal a family secret, they convinced her that her granddaughter was indeed raped by Jason.

"Never seen you at a loss for words, Nana Moira," says Genesis.

"Me at a loss for words? Sweet grief! No, sirree!" she says, and nothing further. She is at a loss for words.

Genesis can only shake his head and leave. For a while Nana Moira remains sitting on the car seat with Blue next to her. Blue looks at her as if to figure out why she is different today, why she is not up and about talking and yelling and joking and cackling with laughter. He also leaves her sitting there and goes to play with his toy truck under the quilting table.

Back at the double-wide, Rachel is sitting on the deck playing the guitar and writing lyrics in a notebook. She hears a roar of a motorcycle. It is Skye. He looks quite different from the way he used to. He's still scrawny in his tight blue jeans and black leather jacket, but his features have hardened and he sports a lush handlebar mustache. His pate is getting bald.

Rachel knew that he must have got her address from Rain. He had only gone as far as the Center before. He is calling her name as he alights from the bike and rushes to the deck.

"You look gorgeous, babe," he says, and reaches for her to kiss her.

Sudden images of Jason on top of her flood her mind and she pushes Skye away. She screams that he must not touch her, and she runs into the house, leaving her guitar and lyrics on the floor. Skye runs after her, pleading with her to listen to what he has to say. She locks herself in her room. Skye knocks on the door calling her name, but she won't come out. He gives up.

She hears the bike roar away, but waits for a few more minutes to make sure he's gone. Then she calls Nana Moira, "Please Nana Moira, I want Blue."

"I'm working, Rachel," says Nana Moira. She is not really working. She is still sitting on the car seat on the porch, brooding.

"I want Blue now," Rachel screams. She is frantic.

"Come and get him."

"You know I can't come over there, Nana Moira. Please bring my Blue to me." She is now sobbing.

She sinks to the floor and wraps her hands around her knees.

Nana Moira brings Blue, and doesn't return to the Center. Rachel has not been in this state in the years that she has been going through counseling. Nana Moira is afraid she may be relapsing.

"What happened, Rachel?"

She won't say.

Later that night Rachel calls Rain: "Tell your bother never to come to my house again."

She doesn't care if that jeopardizes her new relationship with Rain. At the same time she is embarrassed at the way she reacted to Skye Riley. Yes, she does not want to have anything to do with him, but the way she got hysterical was uncalled for. She should have remained composed and told him calmly that whatever existed between them almost four years ago was now history. She can't trust herself anymore. She thought she was healed. She thought she had gained enough self-confidence to face the past squarely, turn her back on it, and move on to the future. Over the years she found comfort in her counselor who started her with what she called exposure therapy, equipping her with coping skills, with ways of reducing her anxieties. She thought she had finally disconnected from the trauma and had instead reconnected with the world out there. She even refused when another counselor recommended hypnosis as a treatment medium; she felt that on her own and with the support of Nana Moira and Schuyler she could finally manage her intense emotions. She should have known better; the fact that she has not gained enough courage to go to the Center and stare at the spot where it happened—as the counselor once suggested—is a clear indication that she is far from healing.

Nana Moira is in the kitchen humming to herself and making a show of washing the dishes that Rachel has left in the sink since yesterday. She makes them clink and clank together so that Rachel can hear that she is doing work Rachel should have done instead of just lazing around at home the whole day.

These are sounds that make Rachel feel safe and content. She looks at Blue. He is fast asleep on the bed next to his mama after a whole day of fooling around.

The following day life returns to normal. It is Saturday. Rachel packs peanut-butter-and-jelly sandwiches and goes busking at the farmers' market for the first time after almost four years. She wants to leave Blue with Nana Moira, but he refuses. He wants to go to town with his mama. She straps him on his car seat and drives her beat-up Ford Escort to the parking lot of the Market-on-State Mall on East State Street.

The old farmers welcome her back. "Where's the bread?" one asks. She does not tell him that although it is pawpaw season there won't be any bread. To bake it she would have to go to the one place she dreads most, and she is not ready for that yet.

Some of the stalls are staffed by new faces. But it is comforting to her that all the produce and products for sale are the familiar ones. It is like returning home after a long journey.

Her spot is now occupied by another busker, a man whose main attraction is yelling and cussing and growling about all the troubles he has seen, while playing a tuneless banjo. The only spot that Rachel can find is further away from the stalls, and she doubts if she will make any money here. Nevertheless she sets up her music stand with a book of lyrics on it, opens her guitar case, and then starts playing.

Rachel sings about the old days when neighbors looked out for one another. If a neighbor saw anyone's child cussing and smoking, she gave him a hiding without minding what anyone else would say. When the parents of the culprit returned from work they thanked the neighbor for spanking their kid. Today it is different. You spank anyone's child you go to jail. She invites the small crowd that is beginning to build to join her in the chorus: "I'm a mama from the hills, I'll spank any kid that crosses my way." She directs this to the kids in the audience and pretends to go after them. They giggle and pretend to run away, and then return to join in the chorus.

This is one of the songs she has been writing since Rain gave her the green guitar. Not that she has any personal experience of the days when any adult could go around spanking other people's kids—or even their own! These are stories that she hears from Nana Moira; she is always lamenting how the world has changed for the worst with "young-uns" disrespecting their elders because they know nobody's going to discipline them for fear of the law.

A severely dressed schoolmarmish woman in the audience takes exception to the song. "You're teaching kids that violence is a good thing," she says.

"All in jest, ma'am, all in jest," says Rachel. "I have one of my own and no one will touch him. Not even me or my grandma."

At this she is pointing at Blue who is sitting near the guitar case, playing with the coins that are beginning to accumulate. A loud-mouthed member of the audience advises the schoolmarm to get a life and appreciate a joke. The rest of the audience laughs at her as she haughtily walks away.

Rachel is not pleased about this. She had no intention of alienating anyone.

It is fall and the weather is good. The farmers' market meets twice a week, on Wednesdays and Saturdays. Rachel has established a following and every week she comes with new songs. They are really more like the ballads she heard Rain and Granny Sue sing. Whereas theirs were a cappella, she backs hers with the guitar and uses her nasally voice for comic effect. She has discovered that she has talent in writing tall-tale lyrics, the same kind she heard Thos Burnett tell, which is also the same kind she remembers her pops telling. Her stories rhyme and leave people in stitches. She is a favorite with the children, and after every session, she returns home with good money. It was a blessing that her old spot was taken because where she plays now is a more open space between rows of parked cars away from the stalls. Her audiences are not stray people who discover her by chance while shopping for zucchini or honey and then drop some change or a single in her guitar case. They are there for her funny songs.

Rachel has become an instant hit at the farmers' market; she wants to spread her wings.

In the meantime, Genesis is giving Nana Moira a headache. He arrives one day at the Center and announces that he and his son have seen a lawyer—Jason wants visitation rights.

"How's he gonna get them in Michigan?" asks Nana Moira.

"He'll be back one day. Michigan ain't the end of the world. He's got to see his son."

"And you think a lawyer will do it for you? You have to win Rachel over, not threaten her with lawyers."

Genesis says it is not a threat. Soon Rachel will receive court process from Mr. Troy.

"I told you, Genesis, you go to the law you lose me."

"I lost you right from start, Nana Moira. You've done nothing to help me and my boy. You saw me come here cry like a baby and you done nothing. Instead you joined the rape chorus."

Nana Moira says she has always been in Genesis's corner because she believes in family. Even after she had been to the counselor and had been convinced that Jason did rape Rachel, she still believed that Blue shouldn't be deprived of a father and family because of it. But if Genesis and his son take her granddaughter to court, she will fight them.

"You'll have me to deal with," she says.

"You've done nothing for us, Moira Boucher. I even got you eighty dozen eggs and you done nothing." Obviously Genesis is not listening to what Nana Moira is saying.

"If you thought you were buying us with those eggs, you can take them back."

"They ain't mine to take back," says Genesis. "But the boy is mine. And the grandson is mine too. God willed it so. You can't battle with God."

"But I can battle with you, Genesis. I warn you. Go to your silly lawyers and take back the case. We gonna deal with this as family."

Genesis shakes his head and walks away.

"I'm warning you, Genesis," Nana Moira yells after him.

A week later a sheriff's deputy serves Nana Moira with summons and complaint. The plaintiff is Jason de Klerk and the defendant is Rachel Boucher. Rachel is away singing with Rain at some county fair in West Virginia, so Nana Moira signs for them. In the evening, after feeding Blue, reading him a story, and then tucking him in, she examines the documents.

Jason is requesting the Athens County Court of Common Pleas to grant him "reasonable companionship and visitation rights with the child currently named Blue Boucher." The complaint states that the child is born of an unmarried mother, Rachel Boucher, and the father, Jason de Klerk, has acknowledged the child and that acknowledgement has become final pursuant to some sections of the Revised Code that are listed in the document. Nana Moira wonders what those sections entail.

When Rachel returns, she sits on the deck and painstakingly reads the complaint and summons. Nana Moira expects a good measure of hysterics or at least a breakdown into a convulsion of tears. Instead, Rachel smiles and says, "I'm gonna write a song about this."

"You need more than a song," says Nana Moira. "The deputy said if you just sit on this, they'll get what he calls default judgment. That means Jason's gonna get visitation."

Rachel takes a long look at Nana Moira standing below the deck.

"Whose side are you on, Nana Moira? You been saying I should let Blue visit Genesis."

"'Twas before they went to the law," says Nana Moira. "And I didn't say Blue should visit 'cause I was on their side. I said it 'cause I'm on Blue's side and he needs a papa."

There is a beep from Rachel's phone. It is a text message from Skye Riley. She reads it, shakes her head, and ignores it. She has been getting a number of these messages lately—Skye begging her to give him a second chance. She only responded to the first one with a curt "don't you ever come to my house again." Twice or thrice a day a message comes in and she ignores it. When she performed with Rain at the county fair, Rachel asked her to tell her brother to stop pestering her.

"Come on, dude, give my bro a chance," said Rain.

"He had a chance and he played with it," said Rachel.

"Damn! You're a tough one. I'll tell him."

Perhaps Rain told him, perhaps not. He continues to bombard her with texts. She will have to change her number.

"We must see a lawyer," says Nana Moira. "We can't do this on our own."

"The only lawyer I know is Mr. Troy. Schuyler worked for him."

"These papers are from your Mr. Troy. We need to find a different one."

The next day Nana Moira checks the yellow pages at the Center and calls a lawyer who advertises herself as an expert in divorce and custody matters.

Rachel and Nana Moira leave Blue with the women of the Quilting Circle, and drive to town to meet the lawyer, Jessica Urbaniak Esq. at her office in West Washington Street. She looks more like someone's grandmother than the lawyer who will get Jason off their back. She sits behind a cluttered desk and shuts her eyes as Rachel tells her story. She is not dozing off though. This is her way of paying attention. Occasionally she ambushes Rachel or Nana Moira with a question that sounds hostile. She tells them she is not about to use kid gloves on them because the plaintiff's lawyer will not nurse their fragile feelings.

"Why did you decide the keep the rapist's baby?" she asks, now looking directly into Rachel's eyes.

"The same thing I asked when I heard she got herself knocked up. No point in asking it now. Blue is here and is a cute baby."

Urbaniak looks sternly at Nana Moira. "Did I ask you?"

She then turns to Rachel and demands an answer. Urbaniak says Jason's lawyers are bound to pose that question because women who raise their rape-conceived children depart from the norm. Raped women either abort or give up the rapist's child for adoption because the child is a constant reminder.

"Why didn't you opt for abortion?"

"I tried; I couldn't," says Rachel. "I was scared, maybe. I don't know."

Nana Moira is surprised how unflinching Rachel is, how she is staring back at the lawyer defiantly.

"I'm not raising a rapist's child," adds Rachel emphatically. "Blue is my child and I'm not a rapist. Blue lived in my body, not Jason's."

Urbaniak is so impressed with this answer she smiles for the first time since welcoming them into her office.

"I don't see Jason when I look at my baby. I see only Blue. My beautiful Blue. Me and Blue both are Jason's victims. That's how I see it."

The lawyer nods.

"That makes a lot of sense to me," she says. "I don't know if it will make similar sense to the judge or to the magistrate who may be assigned the case."

Nana Moira is proud of her granddaughter. This is not the Rachel she knows.

"What I wanna know is how come the law allows Jason to fight for the kid when he is a rapist?" asks Nana Moira.

"I think what you're asking is: Are rapists allowed paternity rights over rape-conceived children? Yes, they are," the lawyer says.

Urbaniak explains that under Ohio law a man who fathers a child through rape has the same parenting rights and responsibilities as any other father, and that includes custody and visitation.

After taking their statements the lawyer tells them what her fee will be. They are both shocked.

"Legal services don't come cheap," she says. "Actually I'm the cheapest lawyer—I mean the least expensive—in town."

Rachel says they will pay. They have no choice because they have to fight for Blue. She has saved some money from the last gig with Rain. She will collect more as she busks on Wednesdays and Saturdays. And maybe Rain will come up with another good-paying gig again. It is the season for county fairs and festivals.

"You're a brave woman," says Jessica Urbaniak Esq. as she shakes Rachel's hand at the door. "We're going to fight this case."

9

Rain sings with Rachel at the Athens County Fair. What is significant about this event is that Rachel is the headliner—the committee invited Rachel and she invited Rain to join her. The two beautiful women are spreading plenty of laughter on the bleachers. They have billed themselves R-n-R.

Rachel is playing the guitar and singing a ballad of her composition in her nasally soprano:

We live in the back of nowhere
At night a train going somewhere
Airborne blast of the air horn
Grinding wheels on iron worn
But ain't no railroad in Jensen no ways
Not since ol' boom-time coal-mining days
Yet the train continues chugga chugga wooo
Haunting ol' Jensen rumble rumble boooo

Rain is playing a tambourine and backing her in her rich alto: *Chugga chugga woooo, rumble rumble rumble boooo . . .*

And then she joins the dialogue:

A graveyard is the place loved by Rain
You ain't gonna be haunted by no train
Dead folk is quiet folk, I tell you again
They're better company than most people I know

The women are prancing about on the makeshift stage when Rachel sees something that startles her. Someone who very much looks like Jason is sitting on the bleachers. It can't be him though. He is in a black suit, a white shirt, and a black tie, and is sporting a beard. She manages to control herself, and continues with the performance.

After three songs R-n-R vacates the stage for the next act. Rachel scans the bleachers but there is no Jason. Now she is really pissed with herself. She believed that the years of counseling had exorcised Jason from her life. Obviously, they have not.

The two women look for something to eat. Rachel gets a corndog while Rain settles for a hotdog with lots of ketchup and mustard. It drips all over her hands as she and Rachel stroll among displays of award-winning pumpkins and enclosures of prize hogs. Rachel wants to go for the amusement rides but the line of shrieking children is too long. They walk past brawny demolition-derby drivers. Rachel kids Rain that none of the hunks will hit on them because Rain is messy and disgusting.

They head to the horse arena and watch the 4-H barrel racing. Genesis's wife rides a shimmering palomino cutting the clover-leaf pattern among yellow barrels. And there is Genesis cheering his wife on. Rachel remembers that barrel racing has always been one of the passions of the de Klerk family. Her eyes fall on Jason sitting some tiers above his father on the grandstand looking ridiculous in his dark suit and sunglasses, and being nonchalant about the race and the cheering crowd around him.

Her eyes are playing tricks on her again.

She tells Rain she wants to go home. Blue is the excuse. She wants to release Nana Moira from the burden of looking after him. Rain wants to take a look at some main stage performers for a while and the demolition derby afterwards. She will drive back home to West Virginia later in the evening. Rachel casts her eyes on the grandstand again, but she can't find Jason.

Back at the double-wide, Rachel says nothing to Nana Moira about being haunted by visions of Jason. Instead she takes Blue to the woods and set up a small picnic of peanut-butter-and-jelly sandwiches and soda. She plays the guitar and sings until dusk sends them home.

Nana Moira tells Rachel about a phone call she received from Jessica Urbaniak. She needs to see her soon because there are new developments in the case. She has another case in Hocking County tomorrow, so she'd like to see Rachel first thing in the morning the following day.

"What new tricks up Genesis's sleeve?" Nana Moira asks of no one in particular.

"It doesn't matter what tricks, Nana Moira. We are going to fight them," says Rachel.

Nana Moira is encouraged by her confidence.

The next day she drives to Rome Township to try once more to talk Genesis out of this silliness. She finds him hand-tilling the garden with a spade.

"We must talk, Genesis," says Nana Moira.

He does not stop working. He is digging a trench, depositing shovels full of soil near the ditch, then digging a second ditch next to the first and moving the soil into the first.

"This is what we call double-digging, Nana Moira," says Genesis. "Best for vegetables."

"I don't wanna talk about vegetables, Genesis. This is serious."

"Go ahead, Nana Moira."

"Stop this silliness of a court case right now. We're like family. We can't hang our dirty clothes out there in Athens."

Genesis stops digging and gives her a pitiful look.

"Your granddaughter ain't fit to be a mother. People have seen her getting drunk and stoned all over the city," says Genesis.

Now this is something new. Nana Moira doesn't know what it has to do with Jason's visitation rights.

"That was years ago," says Nana Moira. "Before Blue was even born."

"So, you see? She was pregnant with my grandson and was getting drunk and stoned all over town?"

"It was the trauma," says Nana Moira frantically. "No ways was that in her nature. She was sick with PTSD—that's what they call it."

Genesis laughs mockingly and resumes digging.

"Now I heard everything. PTSD! She wasn't in Vietnam or anywhere near any war. PTSD!"

"I don't know anything about it myself, but that's what the counselor said. And it was all Jason's fault."

Genesis glares at her as if he is going to attack her with the spade. Nana Moira has never seen him like this before. She moves back a little.

"Hi, Nana Moira," a voice calls from behind her. It is Jason donned in a black suit and looking like the elders of Genesis's church.

"Jason, you're back?" says Nana Moira.

"He was bound to come back sometime," says Genesis.

"I've come back to spread the Word, Nana Moira. How's everybody at the Center?"

His chirpiness unsettles Nana Moira. He missed everyone, he says. He hopes they looked after his compost. Nana Moira stands there dumbfounded. She has no heart to tell him that no one cared for his compost. It just sat there with the rain and the snow and the sun and the wind doing their business on it as seasons changed, until it became part of the backyard lawn.

Nana Moira gets into her GMC Suburban and drives back to Jensen Township like a mad woman. She forgets all about her arthritis and almost trips at the door as she flies in dragging the walking stick. Rachel and Blue are watching cartoons on television.

"He's back! Jason is back!" says Nana Moira, almost out of breath.

"Really? You saw him?"

"I went to Genesis's place and spoke with Jason."

Rachel jumps up with joy.

"That's great," she says.

"Great?"

"Don't you see? It means I'm not crazy. It means I haven't relapsed."

Nana Moira does not understand what she is talking about. She suddenly has a headache. She says she has to lie down; otherwise she will end up being mental like everyone else.

Jessica Urbaniak announces that Jason has upped the stakes. He is no longer fighting for visitation rights but for sole custody. Or, as an alternative relief, joint custody. He has withdrawn his visitation complaint and has filed a motion for custody with the clerk of the court. This is now a different ball game altogether.

This takes time to sink into Rachel's head. She stares blankly at Urbaniak standing in front of her overloaded antique desk and waving the court process. She sinks deeper on the plush loveseat she is sharing with Nana Moira. She didn't want her grandma to be here. But Nana Moira insisted on coming with her. She said she wanted to hear with her own ears what evil the de Klerk family was planning against the Bouchers. Ever since Nana Moira discovered Jason was back, she has been hovering over Rachel all the time like a mother hen. Rachel finds it suffocating. She resents Nana Moira taking over this battle as her own.

"He wanna take Blue from us? How's that even possible?" asks Nana Moira.

"Like I said the other day, a man who fathers a child through rape has the same rights as any father in

Ohio. There are no laws that terminate such rights. If we lived in Michigan or Wisconsin we wouldn't even be here. In those states, and fourteen others, there are laws that automatically terminate rapists' parenting rights."

She outlines Jason's case against Rachel. He says the interests of the child will be better served with him as the custodial parent. He has the means to primarily care for the child; he is a partner in his father's thriving cheese-aging business and a lay preacher of the Reformed Church in America.

"He lies," says Nana Moira. "He told me he hates all that stinky cheese."

Urbaniak continues reading from Jason's motion. Jason states that he is also a musician of note who creates innovative sounds playing exotic instruments. He maintains a stable home that he shares with his father and stepmother, a property to which he will be sole heir.

On the other hand Rachel, his motion continues, is not a fit and proper mother. She is not mentally stable and has been undergoing treatment at the Tri-County Mental Health Services. She is also known to abuse alcohol and drugs, habits that will affect the child adversely.

"So, that's what this is all about?" says Nana Moira. "Genesis mentioned this to me."

"You spoke with him about it?" asks Urbaniak.

"I went to his house to talk him out of this silly case."

"Don't do that again," says Urbaniak. "You're not helping Rachel's case when you do that. Stay away from those people until this matter has been resolved."

"I told you about your drinking, Rachel," says Nana Moira. "See now it's coming back to bite your ass?"

"So it's true then that you drink too much and abuse drugs as they claim?"

"That was almost four years ago. I stopped all that."

"And someone can vouch for you that you stopped those many years ago?"

"The counselors at Tri-County," says Rachel.

Urbaniak returns to the custody motion and tells the women that as the primary custodial parent Jason wants to make sole decisions, or joint decisions if granted alternative relief, about the child's education, religious upbringing, and general welfare.

The hearing date has been set and the case will be before the magistrate and not before Judge Stonebrook. Rachel is relieved to hear this because the judge got Jason off with a light sentence.

The women trudge to the city garage where Nana Moira has parked her vehicle. Not a word passes between them.

"I got work to do," says Nana Moira as she drives on Route 50. And that's the only thing she says until she drops Rachel at home.

"I've got work to do too," says Rachel as she gets out of the car. Nana Moira drives on to the Center.

Whereas Nana Moira finds relief from the tensions of the day by bringing relief to others, Rachel thinks she will find it by rejoining her old friends of Appalachia Active. She does not want to be alone at this point, just she and her music. Otherwise she will relapse, which she fears more than anything else. It's been a long road getting where she is. She will not allow Jason to take her back to a state of anxiety again. She needs the company of people who are working for something good. She calls a member of Appalachia Active, who invites her to a meeting that very afternoon.

She gets into her car and drives to Stewart where the meeting will be held. Rachel doesn't leave a note for her grandmother because she believes she will return home before Nana Moira.

In the meantime, Nana Moira is busy packing goods in her GMC Suburban. She has added another dimension to the Center's services making personal deliveries to the township's old folk. She realized that there were many people not getting assistance from the Center because they could not walk there and stand in line. They had no one to send either. Sometimes a neighbor helped, but in many cases folks were down-right selfish. They only looked after their own. When the plight of the indigent seniors was brought to her attention she undertook to make regular deliveries to them. And these do not only comprise food but also necessities such as toilet paper, diapers, and underpads for the incontinent.

She harnesses Blue on his car-seat and drives all over Jensen delivering the items. This takes the whole of the afternoon, right up to dusk, because she doesn't just leave the items at the door, except for the folks she doesn't particularly like—for instance, those who annoyed her taking the wrong side in the feud between the Bouchers and the de Klerks. For most folks, she knocks, enters with Blue in tow, puts the parcels on the kitchen table, and sits down to gossip a bit, and then moves on to the next person on the list.

It is evening when she hobbles into the last home, a trailer in the woods at the far end of Jensen. She is hold-ing a plastic bag of toilet papers and diapers with one hand while trying to work her way with the walking stick on the muddy driveway. Blue follows with a small parcel of groceries. No one answers when she taps the door with the walking stick. She tries the door. It is not locked. She enters, calling the old lady's name. She hears labored breathing and a groan in the bedroom. The old lady lies on her bed, she is obviously in pain and has messed herself up. Nana Moira immediately dials 911 on her cell phone and asks for an ambulance.

She will not leave until the ambulance comes. She knows that Blue should be home by now. Rachel will yell at her. Nana Moira has tried to call her three times but Rachel hasn't answered her cell phone. Perhaps she is busy practicing new songs on her guitar and the cell phone is recharging in her bedroom. She gets so engrossed lately. She wishes she had not dropped the landline.

Nana Moira bathes the old lady while Blue watches the television. She has to go very lightly with the soaped sponge because the old lady has bedsores. Under her breath Nana Moira curses the old lady's two daughters and a son who left Jensen for greener pastures years ago and don't do a thing for their mother. They stopped caring when she refused to go to rest.

By the time Nana Moira and Blue get home it is way past nine. Rachel's car is not on the driveway. The house is dark. No Rachel anywhere. Nana Moira worries a bit. Rachel never goes anywhere. Not since they took Schuyler away. The only time she travels is when she has a gig with Rain. And she didn't speak of any gig.

Nana Moira prepares pasta with chunky tomato sauce, but Blue has lost all appetite. He had been stuffing himself with potato chips and candy throughout

Nana Moira's rounds in the township. She tucks him
in in the bedroom he shares with his mom.

In the morning Rachel has not returned. Nana
Moira dials her number and the phone rings in
Rachel's bedroom. There it is on a charger on her
nightstand.

Nana Moira's biggest fear is that her granddaughter
has relapsed. Perhaps the visit to the lawyer was too
much for her. The looming custody battle has sent her
head reeling back into the instability of the past.
Perhaps she lies drunk in the gutter in some back alley
in the city.

Her fears are warranted, but for different reasons.
Rachel has relapsed, yes, but not into drugs, alcohol, or
PTSD nightmares.

Yesterday she drove to the meeting in Stewart and
was overwhelmed by the welcome she received. There
were many new faces, but they had all heard of her.
Even though she had not been aware of it, her lone
protests in front of the Jensen Township House had
made an impact. They led to further investigations of
the mismanagement of finances by the township
trustees who were trying to make up for the shortfall
with funds they hoped to receive from fracking companies. All three trustees had to resign, and the township
roads were saved from brine. All this was news to
Rachel.

The activists were surprised she had not known of these developments. She did not tell them these events were likely to have taken place when she was drunk. Nana Moira never mentioned them to her because she is not interested in politics and thinks all politicians are the scum of the earth. Whenever the women of the Quilting Circle gossip about some election shenanigan or about some trustee who has resigned because of some corrupt act, she dismisses the whole discussion with: "Them rascals, they're at it again."

Rachel relished being surrounded by admiring faces of the younger and newer members of Appalachia Active, gratified to receive recognition for work of which she only had a vague memory.

The Stewart meeting was the starting point of a protest march to the hydraulic fracturing waste storage site of Raven-Hunter Water. Rachel learned this was the same company that had the brine-disposal arrangement with the trustees of Jensen Township. This time Appalachia Active was protesting a planned expansion of the site. According to news reports Raven-Hunter Water had applied for a permit from the Ohio Coast Guard to use a barge to ship frack-waste across the Ohio River. The barge would carry half a million gallons of brine per load.

"The river is the source of drinking water for more than five million people in eastern Ohio and western

Pennsylvania," said one of the leaders of the protest march as she handed out posters and placards. Rachel grabbed one of the placards that read *Keep the Frack Out of My Water*. Though she had not planned to attend a protest march and thought she was only attending a meeting, she could not turn her back on folks who thought she was such a hero.

At the site about two hundred protesters converged, carrying signs that read variously *Protect Our Water*, *Science Isn't an Option*, *We Want a Real Hearing*, and *Another Voter for Clean Water*. Others held huge posters of skulls attached to sticks. The protesters crowded at the gate of the site and no truck could drive in or out. The trucks stood roaring impatiently on both sides of the gate.

Rachel led the chant: "How many kids must die of cancer?" and the crowd responded in unison: "Before ODNR wakes up!" ODNR is the Ohio Department of Natural Resources.

Suddenly the spirit of revolution possessed her— she grabbed an American flag from one of the protesters and climbed on one of the trucks. She stood on top of it and waved the flag, which seemed to drive the protesters into a frenzy of chants and cusswords against both the fracking companies and ODNR.

It took all of five hours for the police to arrive, by which time it was already evening. They dragged

Rachel down from the truck and handcuffed her. About thirteen other protesters were arrested. She spent the night in the holding cell, and in the morning she was informed she was being released.

"You're lucky you'll get away with a warning this time," the officer said. "Or you'd be going for arraignment. Next time you'll face aggravated trespassing."

When the time comes for Nana Moira to go to work and Rachel has not returned, Nana Moira finds herself missing Schuyler. She would have just called Schuyler and Schuyler would know where Rachel is.

After she finishes cleaning and feeding Blue her phone rings just when she is about to leave with him for the Center. It is Rachel. She is calling from Jessica Urbaniak's office. No, there is nothing serious, Jessica is not there yet, but her secretary allowed her to make a call.

"Please Nana Moira, come and pick me up."

"What happened?" asks Nana Moira. "Your car broke or what?"

"I left it in Stewart. Just pick me up and drop me there."

"What happened, Rachel? What have you gone and done?"

"I'll tell you when you get here, Nana Moira."

Nana Moira opens the Center for the women of the Quilting Circle, asks them to look after Blue, and then drives to the city to get her granddaughter.

By eight Rachel and Nana Moira are already waiting outside the magistrate's office, even though they were told the hearing would start at nine. They debated whether Blue was required to be there or not. Nana Moira said the law would pounce on them if they didn't bring him along, but Rachel said Jessica Urbaniak would have told them to bring Blue if his presence was required. She wouldn't have forgotten to inform them of such an important thing. Nana Moira dropped him at the Center before they repaired to the Athens County Courthouse.

The two women huddle together on the brown bench upholstered in soft faux leather. It is one of the two placed in the foyer on both sides of the magistrate's office entrance. This must be the courthouse furniture scheme because when Rachel spent hours in this building during the rape case she sat on a similar bench, but on the third floor. The magistrate's office is on the fourth floor.

People come in and out of the offices that open into the lobby. Rachel can spot the lawyers immediately from their dark suits and their look of self-importance. Colleagues meet in the lobby, talk in stage whispers, laugh and pat one another on the back, and rush into one or the other of the offices. Rachel is getting bored. She mutes the volume on her phone and plays *Angry Birds*.

About an hour later Jessica Urbaniak arrives. She looks frumpy in her black pantsuit, a far cry from the glamorous Kayla Trenta, Rachel's image of the epitome of female lawyers. Urbaniak nods a greeting at the two women and enters the office.

A few minutes later Jason, Genesis and his wife, and Mr. Troy arrive. All the men are in suits, including Genesis. He must take this hearing even more seriously than the rape case because he was never in a suit there. Or he just wants to create a good impression on the magistrate. Rachel's heart beats faster as they approach and she thinks her head will burst. But she does not look at them. She focuses on exploding the green pigs by slinging them with birds. She is about to explode the last three pigs in order to unlock the next level of the game and will not let Jason mess that up for her. He will not make her relapse either. She has no intention of breaking down or sobbing or screaming even though her chest wants to explode like the green pigs in the *Angry Birds*. She is a strong woman. Urbaniak told her so the other day. She is a fucking strong woman and Jason better be aware of that. She is here to fight, not to break down.

More pigs explode.

Jason, Genesis, and his wife take the other bench and sit there quietly. They do not even glance at the two women but stare straight ahead. Rachel steals a glance at them. Jason has matured quite a bit. He has even grown a handlebar mustache like his father. Rachel recalls that Skye had a similar mustache when she last saw him. Perhaps that's what makes Appalachian men feel like men. She hates it that a thought about Skye brings an image of Jason in her mind and vice versa. It is an indicator that she is not completely healed. And they are not helping her when they sport the same mustache.

Nana Moira is undaunted. She is staring at the two men, hoping they will turn their heads her way so she can outbrave them. But they never do. They just stare at the wall. Genesis's wife takes a glance at Nana Moira and gives her a sad smile. Nana Moira smiles back and shakes her head pityingly. Genesis's wife returns the gesture and quickly looks away. She is not a bad woman, Nana Moira tells herself. What a pity she is married to an oaf like Genesis. And what a pity Nana Moira has never known her name. She's always been just Genesis's wife since Genesis remarried after years as a widower. She is always just a shadow in the back-ground. Nana Moira suspects Genesis's wife is not in favor of all this conflict between families. But she is too weak to put her foot down and whip these silly men into line.

The bombastic Troy and the dowdy Urbaniak spend a long time locked in negotiations. Finally Urbaniak comes out and calls her client aside. They walk into a library adjacent to the reception desk. Urbaniak tells Rachel that the plaintiff has made an offer. He will withdraw the sole custody claim and opt for joint custody if Rachel signs the agreement.

"No, I'm not signing," she says, firmly.

"You better listen to what the lawyer says before you say no," says Nana Moira.

"It *is* her decision, Mrs. Boucher."

"What if I've a different opinion?" asks Nana Moira.

"I'm afraid you don't count."

Nana Moira has a wounded look.

"Sorry, you do count. But Rachel has the final word."

"I'm not gonna sign," says Rachel.

Urbaniak explains slowly, as if talking to a child, that the plaintiff claims he has damning evidence that Rachel neglects the child while she attends protest marches, gets drunk and stoned, and gets arrested. She warns Rachel that the courts don't look kindly at such behavior and it will weigh against her in favor of the stability of Jason's family. The magistrate, Emma Sussman, is known for taking a firm stand against women who are proven to be irresponsible mothers and has quite often granted custody to fathers and only supervised visitations to mothers. Lawyers who represent mothers hate to appear before her in such matters because they believe she overcompensates. In order not to be seen as a woman jurist who is biased in favor of female litigants, she errs on the wrong side.

Rachel reads Urbaniak's unstated message loud and clear: *Sign the darn document or you're toast.*

"I will not sign," she says once more, even firmer than before.

They never appear before the magistrate that day. A continuance is set and they are given another court date.

In the days that follow Rachel is effervescent. She is singing all the time as she cleans the house or waters Nana Moira's pot plants—chores she has always hated. When everything is spic and span she plays with Blue and teaches him new songs. They sing together. Or she packs a picnic basket and they head for the woods where she continues to sing with Blue. In the evening she writes a long letter to Schuyler, telling her how happy she is, and how she misses her. If only she were here to share her happiness. She does not say what has put her in such a giddy mood.

Nana Moira on the other hand is in the dumps. Her cackling laughter is heard less, and the Quilting Circle women notice the change. They don't enjoy her company as much as they used to because she is either brooding or she snaps at somebody or the other for some imagined sin.

Rachel tries to change her grandmother's mood by taking her to town and treating her to her favorite meal of hush puppies, fish, fries, and coleslaw at Long John Silver's on East State. She buys her other treats too, especially those that satisfy an old lady's sweet tooth. All these efforts fail to impress Nana Moira. She stays broody and tetchy.

She is sitting on an egg that refuses to hatch. How does she tell Rachel the family secret she once revealed to the counselor? Though the counselor long stopped phoning her about telling Rachel, she feels that perhaps that is why things are always going awry for the family—the fact that she has been keeping this to her-self. Rachel's bubbly mood worries her to no end. She prays it is not a ticking bomb.

As far as Rachel is concerned the only thing that ticks is the clock on the wall as she strums her guitar at Donkey. R-n-R has a gig there with a bunch of story-tellers and spoken-word artists. This is not a paying engagement, but Rain does not hesitate to drive all the way from her Blue Ridge Mountains home just to spend some time with Rachel. There is an ulterior motive though. She wants to plead Skye's case once again.

"He's lovesick like a puppy," says Rain as they sit at the table waiting for their orders.

"Then he should go find love," says Rachel. There is no anger in her, which encourages Rain to argue further.

"He found it already, but didn't know it. Now he knows he found it in you."

One of the performers places their lattes and hard oatmeal cookies on the table.

"I don't love anybody."

"You love your grandma, and your friend Schuyler that you told me about, and your baby Blue, and even insufferable me."

"I don't love any man, I mean. Too much trouble."

"My brother is not just any man," says Rain, losing patience with her friend. "And he loves you. Don't you understand that? Whatever he did to you he's sorry about it."

"He says so?"

"He can't figure out what he did to you. But whatever it is he is very sorry and would like you to get together again and he's going to make you a very happy woman."

"Fuck your brother," says Rachel. And then she giggles. But to Rain this is no laughing matter. She loves her brother. And she has come to love Rachel too. They would be great together.

The hearing is held in Magistrate Emma Sussman's office which she has converted into a mini-courtroom. For the gallery there are two benches against the wall at the back. Nana Moira sits on one; Genesis and his wife on the other. They are the only people in the gallery. The magistrate, a petite gray-haired woman with a stern look, sits at a large desk, in front of which there are two smaller desks. Rachel and Urbaniak are at one desk, and Jason and Troy at the other. Plaintiff and defendant have been sworn.

Jason presents his case from where he is sitting. Unlike at Judge Stonebrook's court, there is no witness stand. He outlines his complaint, led by Troy. Parents have a constitutional right to parent their children, he says. He is being denied his rights by Rachel who even refuses him visitation. He loves his son and would like to have a say in the way he is brought up and in his religious upbringing. It is his understanding that his son gets no religious education as he is being brought up by people without religion and therefore without fear of the living God. He, on the other hand, is a member and a lay preacher of the Reformed Church in America, baptized under the name Revelation de Klerk. It is the religion of his ancestors of which he is proud and it is his wish that his son grows up in it. He also fears for his child's morality if he is raised in the Boucher family. Rachel is an immoral woman who gets drunk and takes drugs, as the evidence to be presented by witnesses will show, and she is also a vagabond who spends her time in protest marches or playing her guitar in skanky dives, neglecting his son, and leaving him in the care of an ailing old woman with weak, arthritic knees.

At this Nana Moira utters an expletive under her breath. The magistrate warns her that she will have to leave the court if she can't control herself.

Urbaniak has some questions for Jason. She is brash and blatant. She asks them sitting at her desk and does not pace the floor as Rachel saw the lawyers do at the rape trial.

"You are a rapist, aren't you?" is her first question.

"I ain't no rapist," says Jason with a wounded look.

"You were charged with rape and the jury was deadlocked, is that correct?"

Troy objects. His client was not convicted of rape and therefore it is an insult to call him a rapist. The jury was indeed deadlocked, but the prosecutor did not think it was worth pursuing a new trial because obviously the state did not have a case against his client. The magistrate agrees that it is not fair to call him a rapist if he was not convicted of the crime. But he should answer Urbaniak's last question.

"Yeah. The court found we were on a date. That's why I walked. I thought she wanted to have sex at the time. I accept before God that I misunderstood her 'no' for 'yes.' But I did my time and I want my son."

"You did your time, and yet you were not convicted? What does that mean?"

"It was for assault. Time served while awaiting trial. They said I hurt her major and I'm sorry about it. I'm a changed man now. I spread the Word."

Rachel steeled herself for this hearing. She does not move. Not once does she look at the desk to her left. She is staring past the magistrate through the picture on the wall into the clouds that she recalls covered the sky when she walked into this building this morning.

"As a rapist how are your parenting skills?" asks Urbaniak with a sneer on her face.

"Please don't call me that, ma'am," says Jason.

"Ms Urbaniak!" says the magistrate sharply.

"The plaintiff just now told us that he mistook her 'no' for a 'yes.' That's a rape confession if ever there was."

Troy stands up to make a point, even though he is not required to. He is angry at both his client and the defendant's lawyer. "Once more, Mr. de Klerk was not convicted of rape," he says. "Ms. Urbaniak is taking advantage of his guilelessness and integrity, a result of his religion, to extract from him some false confession."

"And by the way, counselors," says the magistrate directing herself to both lawyers, "we are not trying rape here. I get very grumpy when my time is being wasted."

"We are talking about the safety of a child here, Mr. de Klerk," says Urbaniak unabated. "How safe will this child be with you? Remember you were convicted of assaulting his mother."

"He's my child for God's sake," screams Jason.

"You've already victimized the mother. How do we know you won't victimize her child as well? You're a rapist, after all."

Jason appeals directly to the magistrate. "Please don't let her call me that."

"There is no jury to impress, Ms. Urbaniak. You've made your point."

"Would you agree that any custody arrangement or visitation will force Rachel to see you on a regular basis?" asks Urbaniak.

"I don't need to see nobody but my son," says Jason.

She asks him what he thinks the mental-health impact on Rachel will be if she continues to have contact with her rapist.

"I love Rachel and I love my baby," says Jason. "I won't do harm to them."

After all these questions Troy requests an adjournment. He says he needs time for depositions, and to work on discovery. Jason is still amenable to a settlement and Troy needs time to draft and negotiate the offer. Magistrate Sussman says she welcomes this because in such cases it is in the interest of the child if the parents reach a settlement.

"You saw him squirm," says Rachel as she drives Nana Moira in her vehicle back home. "When Jessica called him a rapist he squirmed on his seat. I bet he pooped himself."

Nana Moira doesn't think there is anything to be bubbly about.

"We gonna win this case, Nana Moira. We'll win it hands down."

Her confidence is boosted even more by a phone call that Nana Moira receives from Genesis the next day. He wants to talk. Even though it is Saturday, Nana Moira drives to the Center to meet him. She does not want him to come to the house because Rachel is likely to hate the idea. Nana Moira does not bother to unlock the building. They sit on the car seats on the porch. Genesis gets right to the point.

"We want you to give evidence on our behalf," he says.

"You want me to give evidence against my grand-daughter. You think am crazy?"

"You ain't crazy, Nana Moira. You'll be doing it for your great-grandson."

Genesis reminds her that she once told him that Rachel drank like a fish when she was pregnant with Blue, whom he continues to call Revelation Junior, and also smoked pot. Who knows, maybe she took hard drugs as well. Maybe she is a crackhead even.

"You idiot man, you're using my words against me?" says Nana Moira.

"Actually, I just came to warn you, Moira Boucher, not to ask you," says Genesis with the glee of someone who has the trump card.

Whether she is willing to take the stand as a witness or not, it really doesn't matter. She has no choice because Mr. Troy is in the process of serving her with a subpoena. Mr. Troy, Genesis adds, is livid that the woman lawyer treated Revelation with so much disrespect in court that now he and the de Klerk family are going to take no prisoners.

10

The West Virginia State Liars Contest is a famous annual event in Charleston. It attracts liars from every corner of the state and audiences from the tri-state area and beyond. Rain has entered the contest and has invited Rachel and Nana Moira to attend the event and listen to some of the best liars of all time.

Rachel is looking forward to the experience. She has not given up her ambition of joining the likes of her father and Thos Burnett as an itinerant teller of tall tales. The Liars Contest is a premier event for great masters of the art. Some of its champions have gained international notoriety in the noble field of lying. There was, for instance, the late Paul Lepp who won six Biggest Liar titles. Today the most revered champion is Bil Lepp, Paul Lepp's younger brother, who has won at least four championships. He is the man Rachel wants to see. She has heard so much about him from Rain.

Rachel remembers a performance where Rain told a story that she attributed to Bil Lepp. It was about Mr. Lepp's idiot savant dog, a cross between a German shepherd and a basset hound. Its sense of smell was so sharp that it could sniff out a four-year-old skeleton in the closet. The dog could smell eggs that Mr. Lepp had eaten for breakfast, then run to the henhouse and bring him the hen that laid them. It could smell spicy chicken wings and a few minutes later would be back with Tabasco sauce and a buffalo. Rachel does not remember the rest of the story—she was laughing so loud that she only caught snatches of it. That is why she is looking forward to seeing in person the devilish mind that is capable of creating such brilliant lies. Rain has told her that though Bil Lepp will not be competing, he will attend as a guest and will tell a story or two. She may even get the opportunity to introduce Rachel because Rain knows Bil Lepp from the church where he is a pastor. Rachel recalls the twinkle in Rain's eye when she said, "It is significant that the biggest liar in West Virginia is a Methodist minister."

Rain tried to register Rachel for the competition too, but was told it is open only to residents of West Virginia. Rachel was relieved; she wouldn't have had the confidence to stand in front of all those connoisseurs of lies and compete against the biggest liars in the industry. She still has a lot to learn.

Nana Moira never goes anywhere. She is not the type that delegates; she does not trust that anyone will do a good job at the Center. But she will go to the liars' competition. Not only will it bring back memories of the men in her life—especially Robbie Boucher who could spin the most ridiculous yarn ever with a dead-pan expression—it will also make it possible for her to spend quality time with Rachel and Blue, something that the counselors said was lacking in their lives. She needs a holiday, even if it's just one weekend. She will also attend an event she last saw when she was a young woman, the Vandalia Gathering, and enjoy the bluegrass music, Appalachian home cooking, and quilt exhibits. Rain has booked them a room at a hotel in Charleston, at a walking distance from the contest venue and from the state capitol grounds where the Vandalia Gathering is held. She will be staying at the same hotel.

There is joy in the Boucher household, but there is anxiety too. Jason's lawyer has requested the court to order a home study to evaluate the living situation of the contesting families. It is their assertion that the de Klerk family will provide a healthier environment for the child—he will run all over the farm, eat fresh veg-etables and live a wholesome life. Genesis has even bought him a palomino colt.

"His grandma will teach Revelation Junior how to ride and barrel race," said Genesis at the previous hearing. He meant his wife who is fast establishing herself as a skilled barrel racer.

That was the hearing that almost broke Rachel down. Troy's investigators had scoured the dives of Athens and found two men who testified that they shared blunts and had sex with Rachel. She did not remember them or the incidents. Urbaniak was frustrated that Rachel could not outright deny their story. The best the lawyer could do was to cross-examine them intensely, to cast doubt on their veracity by exposing inconsistencies in their story. She also aimed to establish that if this happened at all it was many years ago when Rachel was trying to cope with the symptoms of PTSD as a result of the rape. A mental-health counselor and rehabilitation therapist would testify to that effect, Urbaniak added.

That was also the hearing where Troy subpoenaed the police officer who had arrested Rachel at the anti-fracking demonstration. Here Urbaniak's cross-examination aimed to establish that Rachel is a concerned citizen, and therefore a good mother—she had committed no crime; that's why she was not charged.

Before adjourning the hearing that day Magistrate Sussman appealed to the parties to once more negotiate and try to reach a settlement.

Rachel slept for that whole day after the hearing; she was totally pilled out.

One source of anxiety for Nana Moira is that for the first time after many years she will not prepare dinner for the seniors on Memorial Day because that's when she will be attending the Vandalia Gathering and the Liars Contest. She is quite worked up about it. Rachel is trying to calm her down as they relax in the living room, eating cookies, while Blue plays outside.

"Just one Memorial Day, Nana Moira," says Rachel. "Your folks will survive without your dinners for once."

Rachel goes for the last cookie on the plate.

"You can't have that," says Nana Moira, slapping her hand. "You don't wanna be an old maid, do you?"

That's what you become if you eat the last cookie, Nana Moira always warns Rachel. She takes the cookie herself.

"Don't come crying to me when you're an old maid yourself," says Rachel, giggling.

"Duh! Am already an old maid," says Nana Moira munching away.

Blue comes running into the house. He wants another cookie too, but there is nothing left on the plate. He throws a tantrum brandishing Blue, the Amish doll. The two women don't pay any attention to him.

They're used to his tantrums; he'll soon get over it. They pay attention to the Amish doll instead.

"Where did he find that?" asks Nana Moira.

"Oh, it was just lying around my room," says Rachel.

"He's a boy—he shouldn't be playing with dolls."

"It's a good thing. It prepares him to be the kind of man who'll look after his kids. If Genesis had allowed Jason to play with dolls he wouldn't be the rapist asshole he is today."

Blue is so pissed they are ignoring him he flings the Amish doll across the room. Then he runs to his mama's bedroom and throws himself on her bed. Soon he is fast asleep.

Nana Moira is pleased that Rachel can mention rape or rapists without falling to pieces. This is a new Rachel. The old Rachel could never utter a cussword in her grandma's presence.

"Doll Blue is a keeper," says Rachel. "She'll look after Boy Blue like she looked after me."

Talking of keepers, Rachel chuckles at the memory of the last discussion she had with Rain. She was on again about her brother and how he is pining away. Rachel laughed and said he was not pining for her but for what she carried between her legs.

"Your brother didn't want to get it together, but he wanted to get some," said Rachel.

Rain insisted that her brother had changed.

"Skye is a keeper," said Rain. It brought laughter to both of them.

Nana Moira stands to get more coffee from the stove.

"A doll is a keeper, she says. You just wanna mess up Blue's head like yours was messed up," says Nana Moira.

Rachel is pleased that now Nana Moira can actually utter Blue's name without flinching instead of calling him just "the boy" or "the tyke."

"Back in the day boys his age made their own geehaw whimmy diddles instead of playing with dolls," says Nana Moira.

"Geehaw what? I'm glad it's not back in the day anymore."

The mailman delivers a letter, unusual for the Bouchers. The only mail they ever receive are utility bills.

Rachel opens it immediately. It is from Schuyler in Danbury, Connecticut. She is doing well at the Federal Correctional Institute and has learned a new trade. She does the hair of fellow inmates. When she gets back home she will open her own hairdressing salon. Rachel should start getting ready because they will run the business together. Schuyler is going to give

Rachel a few hairdressing lessons and she will be as nifty as Schuyler has become.

Rachel has a searing longing for her friend. She has always yearned to visit Schuyler in prison but Connecticut is far and finances are rather tight. And, of course, the custody hearings have drained her.

She does not say anything to Nana Moira about Schuyler's wonderful plans, though Nana Moira is looking at her expectantly. She continues to read with a big smile.

But the smile soon turns to a sneer. Schuyler is revealing that Genesis paid her a visit in prison. She was happy to see someone from home; throughout her incarceration, she had not received a single visitor. She discovered that this was not just a friendly gesture. He wanted her to give evidence against Rachel. Of course she said no way. A few days later she received a subpoena issued by her former boss Mr. Troy. A fellow inmate, known in her block as a "lawyer," advised her that the out-of-state subpoena could not be enforced. She ignored it.

"They will stop at nothing," says Rachel, and tells Nana Moira what Schuyler says.

"I know. They did it to me too," says Nana Moira.

"They've did what to you?"

"The subpoena thing."

Nana Moira reveals that when she was at the Center yesterday a deputy came and served her with a subpoena. She wanted to tear it to pieces right there, but the deputy warned her that would be illegal. It was a document of the court and she could be charged with contempt.

"Why didn't you tell me?" asks Rachel.

"You got too many things to worry about, my baby."

"So, will you testify against me? What are you gonna tell them?"

"I don't know, Rachel. They say if I refuse I go to the pokey."

"We've got to find out from Jessica what to do," says Rachel and immediately dials her lawyer. The paralegal tells her she is out of town the whole week. She will only be back next Monday. Rachel makes an appointment.

There is a roar of a motorcycle outside. Rachel walks to the door, and there is Skye Riley grinning at her.

"I wanna talk to you," he says.

Nana Moira hobbles to the door and takes a long disapproving look at Skye.

"What does he want?" she asks.

"He says he wants to talk," says Rachel.

"What about?" Nana Moira addresses the question to Rachel.

"Yeah, what about?" Rachel addresses the question to Skye.

"About us. I love you, Rachel. I need you."

Rachel shuts the door and returns to the sofa. Nana Moira follows her. They await the roar of the bike leaving, but all is silent. After an hour or so Rachel takes a peek through the window. Skye is still parked there, sitting on his bike.

The women go about the business of preparing and eating dinner, and then of watching prime-time sitcoms and reality TV. There is no sound of the bike. At bedtime Rachel takes another peek. Skye is still there. Around midnight she is awoken by the roar. At last! But around dawn the roar returns.

When Nana Moira opens the door on Saturday morning, Skye is still sitting there. She shoos him away but he won't budge.

"Am going nowhere till Rachel talks to me," he says.

Rachel is scared though she is trying to hide it. Nana Moira assures her she won't leave her alone while Skye is around.

It is Monday morning and Jessica Urbaniak is briefing Rachel and Nana Moira. The next hearing is scheduled for Thursday the coming week. From what Urbaniak understands, the plaintiff has two final witnesses—Nana Moira who will testify about Rachel's drug and alcohol abuse when she was pregnant, and a church elder from Michigan who will testify about the tenets of the church, Jason's religious upbringing, and his role as a lay preacher of the Reformed Church in America.

"And then we'll present our case. I'll call the mental-health counselor as your witness. Are there any other witnesses you can think of?" asks the lawyer.

Neither Nana Moira nor Rachel can think of any witness.

"Genesis is just being heartless getting Nana Moira to testify to what those ugly men already testified," says Rachel.

"You catch on fast, Rachel," says Urbaniak smiling. "You'll end up taking my job one day. Troy is very smart. He saw how I destroyed those 'ugly men,' as you call them. He fears that the magistrate may doubt their evidence. That's why he wants to reinforce it with testimony by someone who has no reason to lie about you. Your grandma."

"He's an evil man," says Nana Moira. "I don't wanna see him near the Center ever. Something wrong with men, I bet you."

Rachel's mind wanders to another man, the one on the dirt road leading to their driveway. Something wrong with him, for sure. He had parked his bike right in front of Rachel's door for most of the weekend. He only left late at night to take a shower at his motel room on East State and buy something to eat and drink. Then he rode back with his provisions to Rachel's house. Whenever Nana Moira came out of the door he pleaded with her to talk to Rachel.

Rachel was annoyed but at the same time flattered that a man could go to these lengths for her. But she vowed to herself that she would not melt.

At first the women did not allow Blue to play outside. But when he threw a tantrum they had to let him go. Skye whiled away time playing with him.

Rachel phoned Rain who had no clue what her brother was up to.

"Those are the tactics he uses against fracking companies," said Rain. "That's what you guys do— chain yourselves to equipment, sit-in at offices and at fracking sites and refuse to move. He thinks if it works with fracking companies it'll work with you."

Rain laughed and hung up.

When Nana Moira took Blue to the Center this morning Skye was still there. She told him he was trespassing and threatened to call the law. She didn't know why she hadn't thought of threatening him with the law the whole weekend the man was parked in her yard. It's simply that it takes a lot of real serious trouble for folks in these parts to call the law on anyone. They prefer solving problems themselves, sometimes with a shotgun.

That's when Skye moved away from the premises and parked on the dirt road.

The romantic in Nana Moira began to soften. She pleaded with Rachel as they drove to Urbaniak's office to at least listen to what the man had to say. How many women out there wouldn't kill to be pursued so relentlessly by a man? A man with a job to boot?

"There's something more serious that I need to discuss with you," says Urbaniak, bringing Rachel to the present.

Last week Urbaniak and Troy conferred with the magistrate. The magistrate said if the parties did not have a settlement by the date of the next hearing, none of them would like her judgment.

"It became clear to me that we are not winning this case," says the lawyer.

No. Not that the magistrate would grant Jason sole custody. There is no likelihood of her doing that unless Rachel was proved to be an utter junkie who peed on herself. But there is the likelihood that she will grant him some parenting time in one form or another. Maybe even joint custody.

"We need to pre-empt that," says Urbaniak. "Let's offer them generous visitation rights provided they withdraw their motion for custody."

Rachel feels as if she has been punched in the gut. She stands up from the sofa and screams, "No! You cannot play games with our lives! Not with my baby's life!"

"We have nothing to oppose visitation. They presented a compelling case. I don't want to lead you on and you end up paying me a lot of money. Not when I can see already which way the magistrate is leaning."

"I don't care about paying money," screams Rachel. "I don't want my child to have anything to do with that rapist!"

Urbaniak holds Rachel in her arms, and pleads with her to be reasonable for the sake of the child.

"It's a good thing for the child that Jason wants to take financial responsibility. It is in the interests of the child. It's a good thing for you too, Rachel. You'll be released from financial burden. We can go on with the case but at the end of it all the magistrate will grant him some parenting rights."

"No! No! No!" says Rachel, stamping her foot on the floorboards.

"Calm down and listen," says Urbaniak. "I'm trying to help you here. Work with me!"

"That man raped me. He will not be rewarded with any paternity rights over my child," says Rachel, emphasizing each syllable.

The laws of the state of Ohio do not expressly deny rapists parenting rights, Urbaniak explains once more. "We don't live in Michigan or fifteen other states that have laws in place that prohibit rapists from exercising visitation and custody rights over their rape-conceived children."

"Well, I'll live in Michigan then," says Rachel impetuously. "I'm gonna take my baby and move to Michigan."

Nana Moira breaks out cackling. The other two women look at her as if she is crazy.

"You can't go to Michigan," says Nana Moira still laughing. "The elders in black suits, the folk of Genesis and Revelation, live in Michigan. They gonna get you there."

"I'll move somewhere else where they've got proper laws to protect me and my baby," says Rachel with finality.

This new thought brings some tranquility in her.

"You say fifteen states? Which are the others?" she asks.

The lawyer says she does not know off-hand. She vaguely remembers that one of them is Louisiana.

Perhaps California. She can quickly check for her in some of her old files, although she doesn't understand what Rachel wants with that kind of information. It's not going to help her in this present case. She calls the paralegal manning the reception desk and instructs her to look for a file of another case that she had handled a year ago. It takes quite some time for the paralegal to locate the file. In the meantime Urbaniak continues her attempt to dissuade Rachel.

"Just talk sense into her, will you?" she says to Nana Moira. "It's for the good of the baby. Her attitude does not help anyone. Jason does seem like a nice guy who cares for his child. I know many unmarried men who want to escape their responsibilities as fathers."

Rachel will not let her calm be destroyed by the lawyer's reckless remark about Jason's niceness.

The paralegal finally finds the file. She does not return to the reception desk but stands there as Urbaniak pages through it.

"Ah, your Michigan is out of the question anyway," she says. "Michigan is one of the ten states that require criminal conviction of the rapist before termination of his parental rights. Jason was only convicted of a first-degree misdemeanor assault."

She pages through the file again and finds the document she is looking for.

"There are only six states in which conviction is not explicitly required for the termination of a rapist's parental rights. Idaho is one of them. There is also South Dakota, Wisconsin, Oklahoma, and Missouri. Louisiana too. For instance, the Louisiana Civil Code 137 of 2008 reads: 'In a proceeding in which visitation of a child is being sought by a natural parent, if the child was conceived through the commission of a felony rape, the natural parent who committed the felony rape shall be denied visitation rights and contact with the child.' See? It says nothing about conviction."

"But does 'felony rape' not imply conviction?" asks the paralegal.

"It may imply it," says Urbaniak. "Maybe that's what the legislator had in mind too. But it does not expressly say it. You know we take advantage of loopholes all the time."

The paralegal looks puzzled.

"How do you establish felony rape without conviction?"

Urbaniak smiles. She apologizes to her clients; she has to explain to her paralegal because she is always eager to learn. Urbaniak likes that in her.

"Go ahead and explain," says Rachel. "I'm curious too."

"Let me give you an example," says Urbaniak. "A man is charged of raping a woman. The state must prove beyond all reasonable doubt that he is guilty of the crime. If there is doubt there is no conviction. In Rachel's case from what I hear there was a lot of doubt."

"Because Jason lied," yells Rachel.

"Well, people lie in court all the time. Okay, so the man walks free. The woman initiates a civil case against the man for specified damages for rape. In a civil court the standard is different. She doesn't have to prove beyond all reasonable doubt. The proof now is by pre-ponderance of the evidence, which is a much lower standard. All she needs is clear and convincing evidence and the jury finds in her favor. Rape victims have been known to seek remedy through civil action when criminal action failed to convict. This does not happen only in instances of rape. All crimes, including murder. That's why O. J. was found not guilty of murder, and yet in a civil case was found responsible for the wrong-ful death of the victims and was ordered to pay damages worth millions. So, you see, it is not only through con-viction that rape can be established. A civil court can establish rape."

"That makes sense," says the paralegal. "The Louisiana statute would even apply in cases where there has never been any trial at all, criminal or civil, but the rapist confessed to his crime."

"Exactly," says Urbaniak, much pleased with her protégé.

"I should have done the civil case thing then?" asks Rachel.

"Maybe. I don't know the details of the rape case."

Urbaniak studies her two clients. Nana Moira has a puzzled look. Rachel's eyes, on the other hand, are bright and determined.

"So, Rachel, are we now going to be fugitives in Louisiana?"

Urbaniak thinks she is joking. She believes the idea is so outlandish even a scatterbrain like Rachel will not give it a second thought. But, to the lawyer's surprise, Rachel says, "Yep! Me and Blue, we gonna be fugitives."

"Of course, you're kidding," says Urbaniak.

"For real," says Rachel, now really excited. "Me and Blue are going to Louisiana."

"That's the silliest thing I've ever heard," says Urbaniak. "If you don't show in court Jason will get judgment against you. He will get everything he wants."

"He will get nothing. I'll be gone by then."

"How would they enforce that judgment?" asks the paralegal.

"Jason would have to ask the court in the jurisdiction where the child resides to issue an order enforcing our court's judgment."

"And of course another court battle would ensue," says the paralegal. She is as excited by the prospect as if this is her own battle and indeed things will unfold as they are outlining them here. "You may be lucky. The man may not have enough money to go on with this fight in another state."

"Don't encourage her," says Urbaniak, looking sharply at the paralegal.

"Oh, yeah, I will fight that case. In Louisiana I stand a chance," says Rachel.

"I don't want to hear any more of this. In fact, I didn't hear any of it. I'm an officer of the court, remember? I gave you information because you asked for it as my client. I've no idea what you want to do with it. Let's end it right there."

She ushers the two women out of her office.

"I'll see you in court next week."

There is shouting and yelling at the Boucher home. The voices are so loud that even Skye can hear them on the dirt road. At one point he is tempted to rush into the house and intervene. But he is wary of it lest the women turn on him.

At first the quarrel is on why Rachel and Blue must or must not be fugitives. Nana Moira is opposed to the idea of their being fugitives. It is cowardice. They should face the trial right up to the end. But Rachel is adamant. She wants to go to a state that protects raped women and their rape-conceived babies. And Louisiana, according to what Urbaniak told them, will afford her and Blue the most protection.

Blue is sitting on the sofa watching cartoons on television. He holds the Amish doll tightly. When the quarrel becomes too loud he raises the volume so his cartoons compete with the women. When the women calm down a bit he lowers the volume.

All of Nana Moira's yelling and cajoling and begging fail to convince Rachel. Now Nana Moira says she is leaving for Louisiana too. She will not let Rachel go alone out there in the wilderness.

"I'm not going to the wilderness," says Rachel. "I'm going to Louisiana."

"And what are you gonna do there?"

"Don't know. Sing. Busk. Tell tall tales like my pops."

"And who'll look after Blue whilst you do all that?"

"Me. Daycare. HeadStart."

"I'm coming too. Somebody must make sure you and the tyke eat well and are taken care of. That's my job as your grandma."

"What about the Center?" says Rachel. "Many people depend on you in Jensen."

"Been doing stuff for everyone. Time I did it for one of my own."

Rachel gives a last ditch wail and throws a tantrum that could compete with Blue's best performance any day.

"I don't want you there, Nana Moira. You carry too much of the past with you."

"Well, the past is coming along. The past will follow you till you're dead and buried."

Indeed it has followed her, Nana Moira says, eyes gleaming as if with glee. It has followed Nana Moira too. If Rachel must break with the past, Nana Moira wants to be there to help her do it. Nana Moira herself must face some of that past. She has kept quiet for a long time, and the past has continued to eat her innards. She failed to protect Rachel when she was a tyke, she will not fail her again. She will protect her whether she likes it or not. She will follow her to the end of the earth to protect her.

Rachel stares at her grandma. She is trying to understand what on earth she is on about.

"It's about you and your pops," says Nana Moira. "I once found him doing things to you."

Nana Moira cannot bring herself to say exactly what the man was doing. He was touching the toddler in ways that were shameful, using his fingers and his tongue on her parts. When Nana Moira confronted him he said he was merely playing with the child, tickling her to make her laugh. Indeed at first he tickled the child, and the child laughed. But he had gone further than that, and Nana Moira saw it all. She was standing at the bedroom door, the very bedroom Rachel now uses as her own. He didn't know she was there. She warned him to stop or she would set the law on him. He promised he would. But she suspected that given the opportunity he would do it again. It obviously was not the first time, and maybe it was not the last, though she watched him like a hawk ever since. She did not say anything to anyone.

Rachel knew all along something wrong happened in her relationship with her pops. Though she couldn't put her finger on it she had some inkling that whatever it was she was to blame.

"And you kept quiet about it, Nana Moira? You protected your son at my expense?"

"I protected you too. Sweet Jesus knows I protected you too."

"Don't tell me about Jesus, Nana Moira. You know nothing about Jesus."

"I wanted to tell you when you were old enough," says Nana Moira weeping. "It was difficult for words to come out of my mouth. How do you begin to tell something like that? I told the counselor. She said I must tell you, but words couldn't come out."

"Everybody knew except me," says Rachel, laughing. But there is no mirth in her laughter. It is dry and mocking.

"Only me and the counselor."

"Know what, I love you, Nana Moira. I love pops too. I love everybody."

Another bout of calmness envelops Rachel. She is no longer the woman who was yelling at Nana Moira and throwing a fit. She reaches for Blue and holds him in a tight embrace. Blue, on the other hand, is holding the Amish doll in a tight embrace.

"Pops made me a strange child," Rachel whispers. "People said I was a strange child. No one is gonna make Blue a strange child."

"Nothing strange about you. Different, yeah, but not strange."

A tear rolls down Rachel's face and hangs on her chin. But she is smiling.

"Maybe it's a good thing Desert Storm took him," says Rachel, her voice cracking.

"You can't say that about your own father," says Nana Moira.

"I can say it, Nana Moira. And I've said it."

Nana Moira breathes a sigh of relief. She feels liberated. Plus Rachel does not break down, does not explode, does not accuse her of betrayal. Rachel just sits there with a serene expression on her face. It is unsettling to Nana Moira, but it is better than her breaking down.

Rachel gently disentangles Blue's arms and takes the Amish doll. She stands up and gets kerosene from the lamp and a lighter from the kitchen.

"What you gonna do with my doll, mummy?" Blue asks as he follows his mother to the deck outside.

As soon as Skye sees Rachel he blows the horn and waves at her. She ignores him. She places the doll on the ground, just below the deck, and pours kerosene over it. She then sets it alight. Nana Moira stands on the deck with a horrified look. Skye walks closer to witness what is happening. Blue is crying and beating her mother repeatedly with both hands.

"She's burning my doll! I want my doll," cries Blue.

Rachel just stands there, watching the rags burn. She relishes inhaling the pungent smell. There is a beatific smile on her face reminiscent of that day she had set alight baby clothes from Genesis.

When the doll is nothing but a smoldering black heap, she walks to Skye.

"Please go home, Skye," she says. "You make me feel bad sitting here for all these days."

"That's the idea," says Skye. "To make you feel bad. I want you back, Rachel. I don't care if you take me back out of pity or whatever. I just want you back."

"It can't work, Skye, 'cause I don't love you. I don't love anyone but my Blue and my grandma."

"What about my sister Rain? She loves you. She'll be disappointed to hear that you don't love her."

"Don't use Rain in this, Skye. You know exactly what I mean."

She walks away.

Back in the house Rachel tells Nana Moira what she told Skye, and that he won't go still. Nana Moira says they are left with no option but to call the law.

"No, Nana Moira," says Rachel. "They'll arrest him for stalking or something. And then there will be a case and we'll have to go to court. I'm tired of going to court."

"But I've got to go to work, Rachel. I can't leave him here. You never know what a lovesick man can do."

"I'm not scared of him. What more can he do to me that hasn't been done by other men?"

This statement makes Nana Moira even more determined to call the law. She dials the sheriff's office and explains to a deputy about the man camped outside her house.

"We'll send somebody out."

An hour later two deputies arrive and talk with the women. Nana Moira tells them she fears for the safety of her granddaughter with the man stalking her out there. They then go to Skye and ask him to leave. He stands his ground; he has the right to be any place he wants to be. Rachel feels bad when she sees through the window the deputies handcuff Skye Riley and load his bike on a pickup.

The next few days are busy at the Bouchers. The women engage the services of a realtor who will put their double-wide on the market. Unlike a house which has to sit there and wait for the buyer, the sales-man will tow it to a park where it will be given a coat of paint, revamped inside, and then displayed with the other trailers. The realtor will sell the land separately.

As far as the women of the Quilting Circle and the volunteers at the Center know, Nana Moira and her granddaughter are going to the West Virginia State Liars Contest. Nana Moira has indicated to them that chances are that she is not coming back after that. It's high time she retired and looked after her own.

"What are we gonna do without you, Nana Moira? The Center will die," said the women.

"My granddaughter and my great-grandson need me."

She would have liked to have a yard sale but there is no time for that. She donates a lot of the household stuff to the Center for their next Chinese auction. She takes the boxes of memories that were stacked in one bedroom to a storage facility. Rachel takes her car to a park-and-sell lot and asks the lot's owner to accept whatever amount for it, deduct his commission, and send the money to her. She will write to him when she is settled at some motel in the first Louisiana city that they will find welcoming enough to set up base.

The night before they leave Rachel goes to the Center, for the first time since the rape. She walks around the building while she gathers courage to enter. Jason's compost is no longer there. The stack of split wood is long gone as well. She enters the building and walks straight to the quilting room. She averts her eyes so they do not see the spot and goes to the kitchen where she once baked pawpaw bread. She returns, but this time glares at the spot. She glares at it for a long time, unblinking, as if to outbrave it. Then she steps on it and tramples on it as if killing something that is alive and menacing.

She is a free woman as she walks out of the Center.

The following morning the Boucher women and Blue get into Nana Moira's GMC Suburban and begin their journey south. They loaded their suitcases and her guitar the previous night. Nana Moira is at the wheel as they begin the long drive. Robbie Boucher will be with them in his trusty vehicle.

Rachel's cell phone buzzes. It's Rain. She is pissed off.

"How can you do this to my brother, dude? I hear he's in the slammer."

"He was stalking me and I begged him to leave."

"I thought you were my friend, Rachel."

"Nothing will happen to your brother. We aren't pressing charges."

Rain is not listening. She says, "After all the things I've done for you!"

She hangs up abruptly. But she remembers that she is not done with her; Rachel's phone buzzes again.

"The State Liars Contest deal is off," says Rain. "No one wants to see you here after what you've done to Skye. You break his fuckin' heart and then you send him to jail?"

This time it is Rachel who hangs up.

She laughs and says to Nana Moira, "I guess we won't be seeing the great liars of West Virginia any time soon."

Rachel's heart sinks as they leave the Wayne Forest. Yet she is excited to be charting new territory where no Boucher—at least those that are of Robbie's line— has ever ventured. Robbie Boucher's are people of the northeast and when they ventured into big cities it was

Chicago or Philly or even New York. No one has heard any story of them traveling as far south as Louisiana.

Rachel is not fazed by the fact that she is going to be a refugee in Louisiana. She is not scared for her future, and that of Blue's. No one would dare touch her there. She doesn't expect the elders in black suits to give up. They will certainly try to get her extradited back to Ohio. But in Louisiana she will have a better chance fighting them. Her common sense tells her that Louisiana wouldn't dare extradite her child to a rapist when the state protects its own children by denying rapists any parenting rights.

She gazes at Blue on the backseat. He is fast asleep in his car seat. He'll be free too. They were both Jason's hostages. Not anymore.

She wonders why this became her story and not Jason's, why it was the victim's story and not the perpetrator's.

ACKNOWLEDGMENTS

I would like to thank the following for their inspiring feedback:
Elelwani Netshifhire, Jim Shirey, Spree McDonald,
Black Porcelain and Melisa Klimaszewski
(The Sculpture Climber of De Moines)

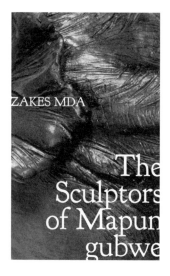

ZAKES MDA

THE SCULPTORS OF MAPUNGUBWE

304 pp | 5 x 8 inches | 978 0 8574 2 095 4 | $21

In the timeless kingdom of Mapungubwe, the royal sculptor has two sons, Chata and Rendani. As they grow, so grows their rivalry—and their extraordinary talents. But while Rendani becomes a master carver of the animals that run in the wild hills and lush valleys of the land, Chata learns to carve fantastic beings from his dreams, creatures never seen on Earth. From this natural rivalry between brothers, Zakes Mda crafts an irresistibly rich fable of love and family. Ageless and contemporary, deceptive in its simplicity and mythical in its scope, this novel encompasses all we know of love, envy, and the artist's primal power to forge art from nature and nature into art.

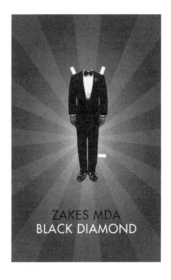

ZAKES MDA

BLACK DIAMOND

312 pp | 5 x 8 inches | 978 0 8574 2 222 4 | $27.50

Kristin Uys, a tough magistrate who lives alone with her cat in Johannesburg, goes on a one-woman crusade to wipe out prostitution in her town. Her reasons are personal; her zeal is fierce. When she receives menacing phone calls, security guard Don Mateza moves into her home and trails her everywhere. This new arrangement doesn't suit Don's longtime girlfriend Tumi, who is intent on turning Don into a Black Diamond—a member of the wealthy new black South African middle class. And Don soon finds that his new assignment has unexpected complications that Tumi simply does not understand. This is a clever, quirky novel in which Zakes Mda captures the essence of urban life in a fast-changing world.